"Did the messenger say anything?" asked Maria.

Harry looked down, trying to gauge the expression in her eyes, but her face was in shadow. "Only that two of your people were murdered in Honduras last week. He told me to tell you to watch out. That Castro has a long arm."

"Then he should take care," she said simply. "He might lose his hand."

Manning frowned. "Are you mixed up in anything, Maria? Anything I should know about?"

She smiled. "Nothing for you to worry about, Harry. Nothing at all."

Manning turned and leaned against the rail again and she stood beside him so that his shoulder touched hers lightly each time he stirred.

She moved close, her hands gripping his lapels tightly, and he held her in his arms.

"Let's go inside, Harry. My next show's at eleven. That's three hours away. We can be happy for these hours."

For a moment, he stayed there, filled with a vague, irrational unease. Then he turned quickly and followed her.

Fawcett Books
by Jack Higgins:

THE DARK SIDE OF THE ISLAND

EAST OF DESOLATION

HELL IS TOO CROWDED

IN THE HOUR BEFORE MIDNIGHT

THE IRON TIGER

THE KEYS OF HELL

A PRAYER FOR THE DYING

THE TESTAMENT OF CASPAR SCHULTZ

WRATH OF THE LION

PASSAGE BY NIGHT

by
Jack Higgins

FAWCETT GOLD MEDAL • NEW YORK

A Fawcett Gold Medal Book
Published by Ballantine Books
Copyright © 1964 by Hugh Marlowe

ISBN 0-449-12802-4

Manufactured in the United States of America

First Fawcett Gold Medal Edition: November 1977
First Ballantine Books Edition: June 1984

And this one for Uncle Bob

1

The Grace Abounding

Manning came awake quickly from a deep and dreamless sleep. It was as if he had come into existence at the moment his eyes opened and he lay there staring at the cabin roof, conscious of the sweat on his body.

He was stripped to the waist and wore a pair of blue denims much faded by sun and salt water. He glanced at his watch and then swung his legs to the floor and sat there looking down at his bare feet, conscious of a nagging pain behind his right eye. After a moment, a step sounded on the companionway.

The man who entered was a Negro of indeterminate age, eyes bright and intelligent in a face seamed and wrinkled by years of the sea. He wore a battered peaked cap, a scarlet shirt and a pair of bright blue denims. Manning looked up and said solemnly, "Seth, who the hell am I?"

The Negro grinned. "One of those days, is it? Maybe you should lay off the rum for a while. I just made some fresh tea."

"Sounds fine. Where's our client?"

"Mr. Morrison went spear fishing on the reef. Said I wasn't to disturb you. I hope he has better luck than he did with that tuna. He sure ain't no fisherman."

"For a hundred and fifty dollars a day he can be anything he likes as far as we're concerned, and don't you forget it," Manning said.

He followed Seth up the companionway and stood with one foot on the rail looking out into the gulf. He was a tall, powerful man with good shoulders. His brown hair was bleached by the sun and there was a two-day growth of beard on his chin. The sun-dried skin of his face was drawn tightly over the bones that framed calm and expressionless eyes.

A two-masted yacht passed a mile out in the gulf on the run down from Nassau, sails bellying in the North-West Trades and a small seaplane crossed to the north, sunlight gleaming on her silver and blue fuselage.

"Jimmy Walker running tourists across to Eleuthera," Seth said as he arrived with the tea. "He's been doing well this season."

"And spending it," Manning said. "Propping up the bar at the Caravel every night."

"I don't think it's the rum that's the attraction," Seth said.

"Sometimes I think you just like to stir up trouble, Seth." Manning emptied over the side what was left in his cup. "Time I went looking for Morrison. We can't afford to lose him. My reputation won't stand it."

"You can say that again," Seth said sourly and helped Manning into his aqualung, buckling the straps securely in place.

"What about a spear gun?" Manning asked.

The Negro shrugged. "You broke one last week, never got it fixed. Mr. Morrison took the other."

"Probably put a shaft through his right foot by now."

Manning pulled his diving mask over his face and vaulted over the side into the clear water. For a moment he paused to adjust his air supply and then swam down in a long sweeping curve.

The sensation of floating in space, alone in a silent world, had never lost its attraction. The sunlight, reflected by the waves, shimmered through gaudy seagrass which carpeted the bottom and shells and red starfish stood out clearly against the white sand in the clearings.

The reef was a forest of coral twisted into fantastic shapes, ugly, dangerous niggerheads rising towards the surface like ruined pillars. A few big striped silver perch chased each other through the coral shrubs. He paused, watching them for a moment, and then swam onwards with a powerful kick of his webbed feet, fish scattering to avoid him.

Beyond the coral, the bottom vanished from sight as he went over the edge. Down in the depths, shoals of rainbow fish filled the deep blue space, rising and falling in a shimmering cloud, changing colour with each movement.

They disintegrated in a silver cloud as several blue mackerel burst through them followed by a shark. Manning was brushed to one side by an invisible hand as the shark swerved by. He rested for a moment, holding onto the jagged edge of a crevasse in the face of the cliff and Morrison swam out of the green mist and started upwards.

In one hand he held his harpoon gun, in the other, the spear on which was impaled a silver perch. Manning swam towards him, and the American poised there in space and brandished the fish. Blood hung in a brown cloud above his right shoulder, drifting in long strings through the green water. As Manning approached, he saw that the upper arm had been badly lacerated by coral.

The American grinned and shrugged as if to say that it was nothing and, in the same moment, his eyes widened in alarm. As Manning started to turn, something grazed his back with stunning force, sending him bouncing against the cliff. He was aware of a blue and silver flash

9

and turned to see an eight-foot barracuda vanish into the gloom.

Morrison dropped his harpoon gun in alarm and it drifted down into the green depths trailing the spear on its recovery line. Manning jack-knifed and went after it, grabbing for the line, pulling the gun towards him. As he quickly reloaded, he could see Morrison vainly trying to squeeze into a narrow crevasse in the rocks.

At that moment the barracuda flashed from the mist and poised perhaps twenty feet away from the American. A second later it was joined by another.

The drifting brown cloud of blood grew even larger and Manning knew that within seconds it would attract more of the deadly fish. He drove upwards, firing at point-blank range into the white underbelly of the nearest one. It twisted in agony, jerking the gun from his hands and rolled over onto its back, tail threshing the water into a white cauldron, blood staining the sea.

Manning swam towards Morrison and pulled him from the crevasse. As they turned, the other barracuda swung in at its mate; lower jaw hanging to expose its murderous, overlapping teeth. The sea vibrated and it turned away, shreds of skin and bone hanging from its mouth. As other slim, silvery shapes darted from the gloom, Manning grabbed Morrison by the arm and pushed for the surface.

They swam through the shallows above the brilliant red and green coral and then the hull of the *Grace Abounding* appeared above them and they surfaced astern. Morrison went up the ladder first and Seth helped him over the rail. When Manning followed, he found the American collapsed on deck, shoulders heaving.

Seth looked up enquiringly as Manning pulled off his diving mask and unstrapped his aqualung. "Run into trouble?"

"Mr. Morrison grazed his shoulder and a couple of barracuda showed interest."

Morrison sat up and Seth examined him, shaking his head. "I told you to watch out for those niggerheads, Mr. Morrison. A man can't afford to draw blood spear fishing.

Most of the big boys, they leave you alone, but not when they taste blood."

"I'll try to remember that," Morrison said.

Manning helped him to his feet. "Let's go below. I'll fix that shoulder for you. Seth will see to the gear."

Morrison sat on one of the bunks, a towel round his shoulders, shivering slightly. Manning took a bottle of rum from one of the cupboards, filled a glass and gave it to him. The American swallowed and smiled gratefully.

"I thought this stuff about sharks and barracuda attacking skin divers was supposed to be all hogwash?"

"Not when they taste blood," Manning said as he gently swabbed the deep cuts with merthiolate. "And another thing. Always reload your spear gun after using it. You never know when you might need it in a hurry."

"I don't think I'm ever likely to forget that again," Morrison said wryly and Seth appeared in the doorway.

"The *Bonaventure*, she coming in now, Cap'n."

"You take over here," Manning said and turned to Morrison. "An old friend I want a word with."

He opened a drawer, took out a flat package and went up on deck.

The *Bonaventure* was an old deep-sea fishing boat, a fifty-footer in green and white, the paintwork peeling from her sides in great strips. The wheelhouse was a good ten feet above the deck and as the boat came round, she dipped alarmingly from side-to-side as though slightly top-heavy.

There were two deck hands, a young boy in canvas jeans, deeply bronzed by the sun, and a thin, balding man with a wall eye. They both wielded boat hooks and as the fenders clashed, Manning jumped across.

In the well, three tuna and a couple of wahoo lay jumbled together, flies buzzing around their dead mouths in great clouds. Sanchez leaned out of the wheelhouse and grinned. "Come on up, amigo."

He was at least sixty, but strong and wiry, his body dried to Spanish leather by the sea and sun. When Manning went up the ladder, he found him pouring gin into a couple of dirty glasses. He turned and offered one.

"Your health," he said gravely in Spanish.

"And yours," Manning replied fluently. "How are things in Havana?"

"Much as usual." The old man turned and spat through the window. "Once we had hope, but now that America has promised not to invade . . ."

Manning swallowed his gin and said, "I'll have a small bet with you. A hundred dollars American. A year from today, Castro will no longer rule Cuba?"

The old man laughed, spat on his hand and grasped Manning's firmly. "How could I refuse such an offer?" He raised his glass. "To Castro, may he rot in Hell."

He took a box of thin cigars from a drawer and offered one. "Maria—she is well? Still on Spanish Cay singing at this club. What is it called—the Caravel?"

Manning nodded. He took the package from his waistband and dropped it onto the chart table. "There's her usual letter. How's her mother?"

Sanchez sighed. "Not too good, amigo. Don't tell Maria. She has enough to worry about." He took a soiled envelope from his shirt pocket and passed it across. "A letter from the old woman. In it, she of course says that she is fine. This is what she wishes Maria to think."

"Still no chance of getting her out?"

Sanchez shook his head. "Impossible. In any case, her health would not permit it." He clapped Manning on the shoulder. "Perhaps next year things will be better, eh? Then you will all be able to come back. You to the business they stole from you, Maria to her home. Things will be as they were."

Manning shook his head. "Nothing stays still, Sanchez. Everything changes."

"Perhaps you are right." Sanchez sighed and took Manning's hand. "Go with God, amigo, and tell Maria to take care. Two of our people were killed in Honduras last week, shot down in the street. Fidel has a long arm."

"In Cuba he may be God incarnate—in Nassau, they'd probably certify him." Manning grinned and started down the ladder. "See you next month."

As he stepped across to his own boat, Morrison appeared on deck, followed by Seth. The American paused to light a cigarette. As he came forward, the *Bonadventure* turned out to sea exposing her name and port of registration on her stern.

"Havana?" he said in surprise. "I didn't know Cuban boats came this far north."

"They have to if they want tuna or wahoo," Manning said. "Since the revolution they've had to rely completely on their own boats. No one from the islands would go within a mile of the place. They have a nasty habit of impounding anything they particularly fancy in the name of the revolution."

"Do I detect a slight edge of bitterness?"

"You should. I have a salvage business in Havana. When the *fidelistras* arrived they took it over along with just about every other foreign-owned firm in town. I only managed to clear the harbour in the *Grace Abounding* by the skin of my teeth."

"You don't care for friend Castro, then?"

Manning shrugged. "He's smart enough. He had to be to promote an eighty-two-man invasion into a popular revolution, but the cracks are beginning to show. He can't last much longer."

"You mean the Russian affair?"

"Something a lot more important from his point of view. The *guagiros*—the dirt farmers. The land was supposed to be parcelled out amongst them. Unfortunately a lot of it's turned out to be virgin jungle or mountain and scrub. You might say the natives are getting restless."

"So maybe you'll get that salvage business of yours back sooner than you think?"

"No harm in hoping." Manning glanced at his watch. "If we move now, we might make Johnstown before dark. You could buy me that drink you promised. Even if we didn't get you a tuna, the afternoon had its moments."

"My pleasure," Morrison said.

As he went below, Seth was already winding in the

13

anchor. Manning went into the wheelhouse and started the engines. A moment later, he opened the throttle and turned out into the gulf.

2

Spanish Cay

It was late evening when they came into Spanish Cay and the beach was a white line of surf fringed by palm trees etched against a vivid orange sky.

As the *Grace Abounding* rounded the point into Johnstown harbour, a deep-sea cruiser moved out into the channel and careless laughter drifted across the water, gay and transitory, blending into the darkness with the muted throb of the engine.

Manning reduced speed and took the boat in towards the crumbling stone jetty that formed the east side of the harbour. A tall, handsome young Negro in the uniform of the colonial police sat on the wall and smoked a cigarette. He got to his feet and grabbed the line Seth threw to him.

Manning cut the engines, reached for his old reefer

jacket and went out on deck where Morrison waited for him. When they climbed the rusty iron ladder to the jetty, the young policeman was sitting on the wall again.

He smiled, showing firm white teeth. "Any luck, Mr. Manning?".

Manning shook his head. "Not a damned thing, Joe." He turned to Morrison. "Have you met Sergeant Howard yet? He stands for the Empire in these parts, or what's left of it. Keeps us all strictly in line."

Morrison nodded. "We ran across each other when I flew in yesterday. How about joining us for a drink, sergeant?"

"A little too early. Maybe I'll take you up on it later."

"You do that," Morrison said and they moved away along the jetty, leaving him talking to Seth.

They could hear the strange, pulsating rhythm of the *goombay*, the Nassavian version of the calypso, as they turned along the waterfront and approached the Caravel. It faced directly onto the harbour and the terrace at the front was shaded by sea-almond trees.

Originally a cheap waterfront hotel patronized by deep-sea fishermen, sponge divers and others whose source of income was considerably more dubious, the Caravel was haunted during the season by tourists in search of atmosphere. The tariff, along with the amenities, had altered accordingly, but most of the original clientèle still frequented the place.

Except for the addition of a small casino, little of the original had been changed. Old-fashioned fans still revolved in the ceiling in preference to air conditioning and the walls contained long, illuminated tanks of tropical fish.

The small dance floor was ringed by tightly packed tables, most of which were already occupied, for in the out-islands it was customary to dine early. A calypso band played on a small dais in one corner beside an archway which was covered by a bead curtain; several couples were dancing.

Manning and Morrison pushed their way through the crowd and the American ordered gin slings. Jimmy Walker

16

was sitting at the end of the bar, a half-empty glass in front of him. He wore an R.A.F. flying jacket with the insignia removed and his old uniform cap was tilted over the young, reckless face.

He grinned at Manning. "Saw you anchored off Cat Cay this afternoon. Any luck?"

Manning shook his head. "How's business?"

"Can't complain. Brought in a full load from Nassau this afternoon."

"How you keep that old Walrus flying I'll never know," Manning said. "What about another drink?"

Walker emptied his glass and shook his head. "Got to refuel at the wharf, I'm taking some people over to Nassau later on to connect with the midnight flight to Miami. Tell Maria I'm sorry to miss her number."

"I'll do that," Manning said gravely.

"I just bet you will." Walker grinned impudently and turned away through the crowd.

Manning offered Morrison a cigarette and the American said, "I'm not sure I care for that young man. Too cocky by half."

"A little young, that's all," Manning said. "He thinks he's in love."

"And isn't he?"

"Who knows? He's at an age when you fall in love with every personable woman you meet."

"A phase I've never managed to grow out of, I'm happy to say." Morrison emptied his glass. "If you'll excuse me, I think I'll have a bath. What about joining me for dinner later?"

Manning shook his head. "Thanks all the same."

"Another time perhaps." Morrison opened his wallet and laid several bank-notes on the bar. "A little something on account."

Manning counted the money and frowned. "We agreed on one-fifty a day. There's a hundred too much here."

"I figure I owe you a new harpoon gun at least." Morrison grinned. "What time in the morning? I'm still set on getting that tuna."

"No need to be too early. I'll meet you on the jetty at eight."

"I'll be looking forward to it."

The American moved away through the crowd and Manning put the money in his hip pocket and ordered a large rum. As he lit another cigarette, the drum rolled and the dance floor cleared at once. The lights dimmed and a spot picked out the archway beside the band.

When Maria Salas stepped through the bead curtain, there was a sudden general sigh as if the crowd had caught its breath. She was wearing black leather riding pants, a white silk shirt knotted at her waist and a black Cordoban hat tilted at an angle, shading her face.

For a moment she stood there as if waiting for something and then her fingers gently stroked the guitar and she started to sing.

She didn't really have a voice and yet there was something there, a touch of the night perhaps, a dying fall that caught at the back of the throat. Probably no more than half a dozen people in the room understood what she was singing about, but it didn't matter.

Manning remembered their first meeting that hot July afternoon. The fishing boat from Cuba packed with refugees, drifting helplessly in the gulf. It had been her tremendous quality of repose, of tranquillity almost, in spite of the situation, that had first attracted him.

It was not that she was beautiful. Her skin was olive-hued, the blue-black hair tied with a scarlet ribbon and yet, in that dramatic costume, every other woman in the room faded into insignificance.

As her song died away, there was a moment of breathless stillness followed by a roar of applause. She took it like a *torero* in the plaza at Mexico City, hat extended in her right hand, feet together. As Manning ordered another rum, she launched into a *flamenco*, dancing as she sang, stamping her high-heeled Spanish boots. She finished on a harsh, strident note that was infinitely exciting.

This time the applause was prolonged. She vanished through the bead curtain and returned to stand stiffly, heels together, turning slowly, her gaze travelling over

18

the whole crowd. As her eyes met Manning's, he raised his glass and she nodded slightly. She gave them one more song and at the end, danced out through the bead curtain still singing, her voice dying away into the distance.

The calypso band struck up another *goombay* and Manning pushed his way through the crowd and went into the casino. As yet it was early and business was slack. One or two people stood at the roulette table, but the blackjack dealer was playing patience to kill the time until the rush started.

Kurt Viner, the owner of the Caravel, was sitting at a desk in the far corner checking the previous night's takings, his manager hovering at his shoulder. A thin, greying German of fifty or so, he wore his white dinner jacket with a touch of aristocratic elegance.

As Manning entered the room, he looked up and waved. "Harry, how goes it?"

Manning took the two hundred and fifty dollars Morrison had given him and dropped them on the desk. "A little something on account. I've been letting the tab run away with me lately."

Viner got to his feet and nodded to the manager. "Credit Mr. Manning's account. If you want me I'll be in the office." He turned to Manning. "Let's have a drink, Harry. Away from the noise."

He crossed to a green baize door in the corner and Manning followed him through. The room was beautifully furnished in contemporary Swedish style, the walls of natural wood panels alternating with hand-made silk paper. A small bar curved out from the corner beside the window and Manning sat on one of the stools while Viner went behind.

"Morrison must be a good client. What's he do for a living?"

"Real-estate or something like that," Manning said. "Does it matter? They're all the same. Paunchy, middle-aged businessmen with too much money looking for excitement. The first thing they do when they get here is unpack, dress like something out of Hemingway, come down to the wharf and expect to have a tuna handed to them on a platter."

"For which they pay handsomely, remember," Viner said. "And in dollars. Such a useful currency these days."

"A fact for which I'm duly grateful."

"You don't like Morrison, then?"

"Thanks to him I lost a harpoon gun, but he insisted on paying for it and he knows I'm insured. I suppose he's better than most."

"He must be. Two hundred and fifty dollars is a fair day's pay by any standards." Viner hesitated and then said slowly, "You know, your credit's always good here, Harry, but it's quite obvious you aren't even making a living at the moment."

"Have you got a better suggestion?"

The German refilled his glass and said slowly, "You go to Miami occasionally, don't you?"

Manning nodded. "So what?"

"The *Grace Abounding* is a good-sized boat. You could carry passengers."

Manning frowned. "You mean Cuban refugees? Illegal immigrants? Have you any idea what the penalties are?"

"The rewards could be high."

"You're telling me. Five years in gaol. That coast is alive with small naval craft, especially since the Cuban crisis. What's your interest, anyway? You don't need that kind of money."

"You could say I have an affinity for refugees. I was one myself for several years after the war." Viner smiled. "Think it over, Harry. The offer is still open."

Manning emptied his glass and stood up. "Thanks all the same, but things aren't quite *that* tough. See you later."

He left the room and went through the casino ino the bar. For a moment he hesitated and then went out into the foyer past the reception desk and mounted the stairs to the first floor.

He was immediately conscious of the quiet. He passed along the broad, carpeted corridor and somewhere a woman laughed, the sound of it curiously remote. The music from below might have come from another world.

He opened the door at the end of the corridor and went in. The room was a place of shadows, one shaded lamp standing on a small table in the centre. The french windows stood open to the terrace, the curtain lifting slightly in the wind as he crossed the room.

She was sitting in the darkness in an old wicker chair, a robe wrapped closely about her against the chill of the night air.

"Hello, Harry!" she said softly.

He gave her a cigarette. As the match flared in his cupped hand, she leaned forward, the lines of her face thrown sharply into relief, the eyes dark pools.

"What kind of a day have you had?"

"No worse than usual. It's a great life if you don't weaken."

He was unable to keep the bitterness from his voice and she shook her head. "You can't go on like this, Harry, brooding about the past. You had a thriving business once in Havana, but you lost it. Why can't you accept that instead of living from day to day hoping for some miracle to give it back to you."

"Nobody's having to support me," he said. "I'm making a living."

"Only just." There was an edge of anger in her voice. "What kind of a life is this for a man like you? You started in Havana with nothing. Why can't you start again?"

"Maybe I'm tired," he said. "I'm fifteen years older, remember. I've just been talking to Viner. He wants me to start running refugees into Florida. A quick passage by night and no questions asked."

She leaned forward in alarm. "You didn't accept?"

"Don't worry," he said. "I've still got that much sense left." He took the envelope from his shirt pocket and dropped it onto her lap. "A letter from your mother."

She got to her feet with a slight exclamation and hurried into the bedroom. He watched her feverishly tear open the envelope in the light of the lamp and turned away, leaning on the rail.

After a while she came back outside and stood beside him. "How was Sanchez?"

"Seemed pretty fit to me."

"Did he say anything?"

He looked down, trying to gauge the expression in her eyes, but her face was in shadow. "Only that two of your people were murdered in Honduras last week. He told me to tell you to watch out. That Castro has a long arm."

"Then he should take care," she said simply. "He might lose his hand."

Manning frowned. "Are you mixed up in anything, Maria? Anything I should know about?"

She smiled. "Nothing for you to worry about, Harry. Nothing at all."

Manning turned and leaned against the rail again and she stood beside him so that his shoulder touched hers lightly each time she stirred. The wind was freshening off the water and a light mist rolled across the harbour. He felt at peace and restless, happy and discontented, all at the same time. It had been a bad day and the past came too easily to mind. He sighed and straightened.

She looked up, her face a white blur in the darkness. "What are you thinking about?"

"Life!" he said. "How you can never be sure about anything. Not really."

She moved close, her hands gripping his lapels tightly, and he held her in his arms. Out beyond the point, the sea was beginning to lift into whitecaps.

"Storm before morning," he said.

She looked out to sea and shivered. "Let's go inside, Harry. My next show's at eleven. That's three hours away."

She gently pulled herself free and went in. For a moment, he stayed there, looking out to sea and then a small wind moaned eerily as it slid over the rooftop, filling him with a vague, irrational unease. He turned quickly and followed her.

He lay there, caught between the shadowy lines of sleep and waking for quite some time, aware that the wind had strengthened and somewhere far out to sea a single clap of thunder echoed hollowly.

After a while, he stretched out a hand and realized that he was alone. He threw back the bedclothes and reached for his watch. It was just after eleven. For a moment, he sat there frowning and then remembered that it was Friday and she had a late show. She'd obviously decided not to waken him.

He got to his feet, padded across to the bathroom and turned on the shower. The cold stinging lances of water invigorated him and by the time he was dressed his body was glowing and alive.

It was eleven-thirty when he went downstairs and the wind was rattling the shutters of the windows along the terrace. There were still a few people in the casino, but the bar was strangely deserted.

Morrison was sitting on a high stool, drinking a gin sling and leafing through an old yachting magazine. He looked up and smiled. "Hello there. How about a drink?"

Manning looked down at the deserted dance floor with a frown. "What's happening around here? When did the show finish?"

"There wasn't a late show tonight," Morrison said and a sudden gust of wind rattled the front of the building. "Looks like we're in for a blow."

As Manning started to turn, that vague, irrational unease moving inside him again, Viner came in from the casino carrying a cash box. As he started to go behind the bar, Manning caught him by the arm.

"What in hell's going on here? Maria told me she had another show at eleven. Where is she?"

Viner put the cash box down on the bar and sighed heavily. "Maybe you'd better have a drink, Harry."

Before Manning could reply, a cry sounded outside and the front door burst open, a gust of wind sending it crashing back against the wall.

The man who staggered in had been running hard and his oilskin coat streamed water. He grabbed for the edge of the bar and leaned against it, moaning softly.

He was an old deep-sea fisherman called Saunders who

ran a charter boat during the season. Viner went behind the bar, poured rum into a glass and pushed it across.

"Drink that and pull yourself together. What's happened?"

"Jimmy Walker's gone down in the sea in that old plane of his." Saunders swallowed some of the rum and coughed. "I was about two miles out close by Blackstone Reef. There's a sea like a mill race running out there."

"Never mind that," Manning said. "What happened?"

"Search me. There was one hell of a bang. When I looked up, she fell into the water like a stone."

"Didn't you go back to help?" Morrison demanded.

"In my old tub? Mister, the way that sea's running I'd all on to get in here in one piece. I figured the best thing to do was to get some help—real help."

There was a sudden crash as Viner dropped the rum bottle he was holding. He swayed slightly, his face very white, and steadied himself against the bar.

"For God's sake, pull yourself together," Manning told him. "Grab a coat and let's get out of here."

"But you don't understand, Harry," Viner said. "Maria was on that plane."

Manning stood there gazing at him, the coldness flooding through him. At that moment, the heavens opened with a clap of thunder and rain started to rattle against the roof.

3

Dark Waters

It was raining hard as the *Grace Abounding* left the shelter of the harbour and turned out to sea. Manning opened the throttle wide and she lifted to meet the waves with a surge of power that left Joe Howard in his old police launch far behind.

Manning felt strangely calm, pushing all other possibilities from his mind except the one that they would get there in time to do some good. He fumbled for a cigarette and Morrison handed him one quickly and offered a light.

"What kind of a chance have they got?"

"Pretty good," Manning said. "It'll take a lot to sink that old Walrus and Jimmy carries a full complement of dinghies and so on in case of ditching. He was strict about things like that. Came from his R.A.F. training, I suppose."

"What about this reef where they came down?"

"The one thing I'm worried about."

Old Saunders removed his pipe and nodded. "The sea can play strange tricks out there when the weather gets rough."

As the *Grace Abounding* rose to the crest of a wave, a sudden squall hit her broadside on and the whole boat shuddered and slid sideways into the valley below.

Morrison and Saunders were thrown violently to one side and Manning grabbed for the wheel as it spun and brought her round in time to meet the next wave as it lifted to meet them.

In the light from the binnacle, Morrison looked sick and frightened. "Does that happen often?"

"Usually not more than once," Manning said dryly.

The door of the saloon opened, light flooding out, and Seth came up the companionway carrying a jug of tea and a mug. "Man, but there's a sea running tonight."

"You can say that again," Morrison told him. "How's Viner?"

"Sick to his stomach as usual. We might as well have left him on dry land."

Manning swallowed some of the scalding tea and passed the mug to Saunders. The red and green navigation lights cast a strange glow over the deck and beyond, nothing existed except the sea and the night.

A few moments later, it stopped raining and the moon appeared in a patch of clear sky between clouds that moved smoothly across the sky. The wind died and the squall was over as suddenly as it had begun.

In the moonlight, the sea stretched to the horizon and the *Grace Abounding* slid across great heaving swells smoothly, her prow biting into the water. Above the roar of the engine, a hollow booming sounded and a white fountain of water lifted fifty feet into the night.

"What in hell was that?" Morrison demanded in alarm.

"A blow-hole," Saunders said. "Always happens in bad weather. The reef's hollow underneath."

Conversation died as they approached. Waves rolled in to dash upon the great, jagged black rampart that towered thirty feet above the sea. An undertow sucked at them as Manning started to turn to port and here was a hollow slapping sound against the keel of the boat. At one side, the water broke into spray, foaming high into the air, while all around, white patches appeared as jagged rocks showed through.

As he throttled down, the steering became increasingly sluggish and they drifted in towards a great green slab of rock. Manning and Seth heaved on the wheel together and they were round the southern tip of the reef and into the comparative shelter of the lee side.

The sea stretched away into the night, surrounding rocks and cays clearly visible in the bright moonlight. There was no sign of the Walrus. Seth opened the front window and Manning switched on the spot and turned it slowly, the beam splaying across the water towards the reef.

Saunders called out excitedly and pointed. Caught in the light of the beam was a section of silver fuselage. Seth ran to the stern to throw out the anchor and Manning switched off the engine. Morrison and Saunders had gone up on deck. As Manning followed, the American gave a cry of horror.

Manning climbed on top of the wheelhouse and turned the spot and his stomach heaved. In the harsh white light, the sea boiled as dozens of sharks plunged and fought like mad dogs over a piece of meat. One great ugly head lifted out of the water, a human arm clamped between its teeth, before plunging down to escape the attentions of three others.

Manning jumped to the deck and ran into the cabin. When he came back he was carrying a Garand automatic carbine. He stood at the rail, bitter, impotent anger rising inside him, and pumped round after round into the gleaming bodies.

It was all to no purpose. The sea boiled over in a white cauldron as those who struggled in their death agony, thrashing the water in fury, became in turn the victims.

Blood fountained up, lumps of raw flesh drifted on top of the water, the sharks twisted and turned until the whole thing was like something out of a terrible nightmare and the sea itself seemed to cry out in agony.

As the last shot echoed flatly across the water, Manning threw the useless carbine to the deck and stumbled below. For a little while, the others stood there looking helplessly at each other and then Seth went into the wheelhouse and turned off the spot.

Manning sat at the table in the saloon smoking a cigarette, an empty glass in front of him. He reached for the bottle and the door opened and Viner came in. He closed it quickly and slumped down in the opposite chair. His hair was soaked by the rain and he looked very pale.

"What's it like out there?" Manning said calmly. "Have they finished yet?"

Viner shook his head and buried his face in his hands. Manning half-filled his glass with rum and pushed it across.

"Drink some of that. You'll feel better."

Viner shook his head. "I don't think so. I'd rather have a cigarette."

Manning gave him one and the German lit it carefully, coughing as the smoke caught at the back of his throat. It was very quiet there in the saloon with the spray spattering lightly against the windows.

After a while, Manning said, "Where was she going—Miami?"

Viner nodded. "She had a letter from the Cuban refugee people there. They wanted her to go on tour in the States to raise money for their organization."

"But why go without telling me?"

"She thought it would be best that way. A clean break."

Manning shook his head. "I don't get it. I don't get it at all. There must have been some other reason. Something that makes sense."

"All right, Harry," Viner said. "I'll give it to you straight. Ever since you arrived on Spanish Cay you've been drowning in a sea of self-pity. You seemed to think you were the only one to take a knock over the Cuban affair. And then Maria came along. At least she managed to stop you from drinking yourself into the grave, but ever since, you've used her like a crutch. She decided it was time you learned to walk on your own two feet again."

Manning sat there staring at him, a slight frown on his face and then he emptied his glass, got up and went outside. Saunders, Morrison and Seth were talking quietly in the wheelhouse and he brushed past them and went and stood at the rail, thinking about her down there in the dark water, knowing that everything Viner had said was true.

Gradually a faint pearly luminosity appeared and he was able to distinguish the greyness of the mist curling up from the water and the dark, silver lances of the rain.

The nightmare was over. The sea lifted in a slight swell, creaming against the base of the reef. The blowhole was silent. The sharks had gone.

The police launch was anchored twenty or thirty yards to port and Joe Howard emerged from the wheelhouse and raised an arm. He dropped over the stern into his dinghy, cast off and sculled across.

When he climbed over the rail, his normally good-humoured face was grave. "I've radioed Nassau. They're sending a salvage boat and a couple of divers. Should be here about noon."

Manning shook his head. "There was no need. I'm going down myself."

"Don't be a fool, Harry!" Viner said sharply as he emerged from the wheelhouse followed by the others.

"It's my neck."

Seth shook his head and said softly, "Nothing for you down there, Harry. Maybe a tiger shark or two hoping for something the others missed, but it ain't likely."

"I'll see for myself." Manning turned to Howard. "Sorry, Joe, but that's the way it is."

The young policeman sighed and said to Seth, "Get your spare aqualung ready while you're about it. I'll go down with him." He grinned tiredly at Manning. "I *am* supposed to be in charge here in case you'd forgotten."

"Are you two crazy or something?" Morrison said.

Manning ignored him and started to take off his shoes and outer clothing. As Joe Howard followed his example, he smiled reassuringly at the American. "Don't worry,

29

Mr. Morrison. We've done this sort of thing before."

They kept on shirts and pants as some protection against the coldness of the water. When Seth brought the equipment up from the saloon, he and Saunders helped them into it quickly.

No one bothered to talk. For Manning, there was a desperate unreality about everything. It was a bad dream. A dream from which he might awaken at any moment, stretch out his hand in the darkness and find her there beside him.

When he went over the rail, the sharp coldness of the water was like a physical blow, bringing him back to reality. He hovered just below the surface to adjust his air supply and went down through the opaque grey water without waiting for his companion.

The plane loomed out of the shadows almost at once. It had settled on a bank of sea grass which stretched to the base of the reef and as he swam towards it he was aware of the undertow tugging at his body, pulling him towards the great rock face and the caverns beneath.

The main fabric of the Walrus was still intact, but the tail and the baggage compartment had completely disappeared leaving a great ragged hole at one end of the fuselage, the metal twisted and blackened as if by some tremendous explosion. As Manning hovered beside it, Joe Howard arrived.

There was a slight frown on the Negro's face and he looked worried. Manning patted him on the shoulder reassuringly and they swam inside. The seats were still there and the door to the pilot's cabin swung gently in the current, but there were no bodies. The passengers and crew had vanished without trace.

Howard went into the cabin and Manning swam outside and waited for him, clinging to the fuselage. The sun was rising and the first pale rays slanted down through the grey water, but there was still that strange absence of life.

Seth had been right. There was nothing for him here. Maria Salas had vanished along with her companions as completely as if she had never existed. He was about to kick out towards the surface when Joe appeared beside him and tapped him on the shoulder.

He pointed to the pale fronds of the sea grass that stretched towards the base of the reef, pulled by the undertow. Manning realized at once what he meant. Over the years, the action of the sea had scoured away the base of the cliff, creating a great cavern underneath. There was always the possibility that one or more of the bodies, caught in the undertow, had been sucked inside before the sharks could get at them.

He let go of the plane, moving towards the base of the cliff, and the current pulled him along. The entrance was a dark slash in the rock no more than three feet high and he ducked inside and waited for Joe Howard to join him.

The cave was full of small, rainbow-coloured fish and arched above his head like a cathedral. The early morning sun streamed out of the blow-hole in the roof and filtered down through the water in great translucent rays.

It was strangely peaceful and somehow cut off from the world outside and then Joe Howard appeared beside him and the cloud of fish disintegrated in alarm, exposing a body pinned to the roof of the cavern.

It was Jimmy Walker. He was wearing an inflated life-jacket and floated there against the roof, face down. His eyes were closed, his limbs perfectly relaxed. There was no mark on him anywhere. Manning and Howard rose together, the fish scattering to avoid them. They each took an arm and swam back towards the entrance.

They paused at twenty feet for several minutes to decompress and surfaced slightly astern of the *Grace Abounding*. Saunders was the first to see them. He cried out excitedly and the sound died in his throat as he saw their burden.

Seth had put the ladder over the side in readiness and he came down it quickly and took a firm grip on Walker's life-jacket. Morrison leaned over to help him. When Manning climbed over the rail, the body was laid on its back beside the wheelhouse.

"Not a mark on him," Saunders said in awe. "How come they missed him?"

Manning pushed up his mask and spat out his rubber mouth-piece. "We found him under the reef. He must have still been at the controls when the plane touched bottom. That undertow must have been tremendous last night. The moment he emerged from the cabin, it would have taken him straight under."

"How come his life-jacket's inflated?"

"Probably a reflex action as he went under. Maybe he realized what was happening and hoped to come up through the blow-hole."

He shivered, thinking of Jimmy Walker down there in the darkness with no one to help him, and Morrison said, "What about the others?"

"Nothing left to find," Joe Howard told him. "Looked to me as if there'd been some sort of an explosion."

The American frowned. "What was it? One of the engines?"

Joe Howard shook his head. "Whatever it was, it was in the baggage compartment. Blew the tail clean off. She must have gone down like a stone."

There was a sudden silence and Saunders drew in his breath. After a moment, Seth said slowly, "You mean it wasn't no accident, Joe?"

Manning dropped his aqualung to the deck, picked up a towel and draped it across Jimmy Walker's face. When he straightened, he looked incredibly calm.

"That's exactly what he means," he said.

4

A Man Called Garcia

When Manning opened the door the bed was still rumpled and unmade as he had left it and he moved across and gently touched the dent in the pillow where her head had lain. He shivered involuntarily and opened the french windows, allowing the early morning sun to come flooding in.

He searched the room thoroughly, starting with the wardrobe and going through every drawer and cupboard. He found plenty of his own things, but there was nothing of hers. Not even a handkerchief. It was as if she had never existed.

He stood there listening to the stillness for a moment and then stripped to the waist, went into the bathroom and washed the salt from his face and body. He was pulling a clean shirt over his head when the door opened and Joe Howard came in.

He sat on the end of the bed and took a slip of paper from the breast pocket of his tunic. "I've got the passenger list here. There were only four of them: Maria, an American businessman called Fallon, Mrs. Norah Hamilton, an English tourist, and a man called Perez."

Manning turned slowly, a slight frown on his face. "Cuban?"

"He was staying at the Old Ship Tavern. Been here for maybe two weeks. Small, middle-aged man with a walkingstick."

Manning nodded. "I remember him. Limped badly on his right foot."

"It wasn't surprising," Howard said. "He was lucky to have one. A Castro agent tossed a bomb at him in Vera Cruz a couple of months back. Real name was Dr. Miguel de Rodriguez, a prominent Cuban refugee. He'd been having too much success in the Central American states whipping up opposition to the Castro régime."

"What was he doing here?"

"Recuperating quietly, which explains the assumed name. Nassau informed me as a matter of course when he came in. I didn't know he was leaving last night. Obviously someone else did."

"And planted a bomb in the baggage compartment?"

"Easily enough done. The Walrus was moored out there beyond the point on her own for several hours after dark. Hard luck on the other passengers, but then I suppose these people never give that side of it a thought."

Manning found that his hands were trembling. He lit a cigarette and stood at the window. "What happens now?"

"The Commissioner wants me in Nassau right away. With luck I should be back by this evening. I'll let you know if anything turns up." He moved to the door and hesitated. "She was a nice girl, Harry. I'm sorry! Damned sorry!"

The door closed softly behind him and Manning stayed there looking out across the harbour for a while, thinking about it all, and then he reached for his cap and went downstairs.

The bar was deserted and he went out on the terrace

and found Viner having a late breakfast on his own. The German snapped his fingers for the waiter as Manning joined him.

"What about some breakfast, Harry?"

Manning shook his head. "Just coffee."

The waiter brought another cup, filled it and retired. Viner continued with his meal, obviously embarrassed, and Manning lit a cigarette and looked over the water at the dim bulk of Andros shimmering in the heat haze.

Viner finished eating and carefully fitted a cigarette into an elegant silver holder. "Your coffee's getting cold."

Manning emptied his cup and helped himself to some more. "Where's Morrison? I was supposed to be taking him out at the crack of dawn."

"Under the circumstances, he didn't think you'd be interested. Decided to take a run across to Nassau. Joe gave him a lift in the police launch."

"Did he tell you about Rodriguez?"

The German nodded. "It doesn't make sense, Harry. To kill a man they think their enemy is one thing, but this sort of affair can only do their cause harm."

"Maybe they want to put a little fear into all of us," Manning said. "Show us they mean business. I think Joe was wrong about the way they planted that bomb, though."

Viner looked surprised. "I thought his theory seemed pretty sound."

"So did I at first, but I've been thinking about it. Jimmy Walker always supervised loading himself. He had a thing about it ever since one of his shipping clerks tried to run a little heroin into Vera Cruz and Jimmy nearly took the drop for it. And he always locked that luggage compartment. He'd have noticed if anyone had tampered with that door."

"Then the bomb must have been taken on board in someone's luggage. Probably by Rodriguez himself."

Manning nodded. "Whoever it was wouldn't know a thing about it. Probably planted at their hotel. Lots of people would have the opportunity. Chambermaids, waiters and so on. I shouldn't have thought Rodriguez would

35

have fallen for a thing like that, though. A man in his position only survives by being careful."

"Obviously he wasn't careful enough," Viner said dryly. "But even if the bomb was planted in another passenger's luggage, it shouldn't be too difficult to find the culprit. We could start by checking on all staff taken on by the hotels in question during the past fortnight."

"A good point," Manning said. "Was anyone on that list staying here?"

Viner shook his head. "We know Rodriguez was at the Old Ship Tavern. We could make some enquiries there for a start. You know the owner, Bill Lumley, as well as I do. He'll help in any way he can."

Manning swallowed the rest of his coffee and stood up. "I've got a better idea. You go see Bill. I'll call at the shipping office and ask them for another copy of that passenger list. That'll tell us where the other two were staying."

Viner nodded. "I'll meet you at the Old Ship then. What about the police?"

Manning shrugged. "Joe won't get back till late this afternoon. Our bird could have flown the coop by then. I wouldn't like that to happen."

"I don't think I should, either," Viner said.

Manning left him there, went down the steps and turned along the waterfront. Seth was sitting on the sea wall talking to two sailors. He jumped down and crossed the dusty road.

"We going out today, Harry?"

Manning shook his head. "I don't think so."

He felt as if he were under deep water and everything seemed to move in slow motion. All sounds were muffled and far off. Even his own voice seemed to belong to a stranger and again he had that peculiar feeling that it was only a dream. That somehow he would wake up and that everything would be different.

The shipping office was dark and cool when he went inside. The Negro clerk was drinking a glass of ice-water and he put it down hastily, his face sober.

"What can I do for you, Mr. Manning?"

36

"I'd like a look at that passenger list," Manning said. "The one you showed Sergeant Howard."

As the clerk started to search through a mass of papers, the door at the rear opened and a young Negro entered. As he took off his jacket, the first man found what he was looking for.

"This is it, Mr. Manning. This is the one Sergeant Howard took a copy of. 'Course I didn't make the original out. That was Bill here. He's the night man."

Bill moved forward, glanced at the passenger list and nodded. "That's it, Mr. Manning. That's the final copy I made after Mr. Walker left."

"Final copy?" Manning said. "What's that supposed to mean?"

"Well, sometimes people don't show up for the flight," the Negro explained. "When that happens we miss them off the final copy."

Manning felt a coldness inside him. In that single instant, everything jumped back into focus. He leaned across the counter and said carefully, "Did someone fail to make the flight last night?"

The Negro nodded. "A Mr. Garcia. He booked his seat around noon, but didn't show up at flight time."

"And what about his luggage?"

"Oh, that was on the plane. I told him it had to be here by seven. Mr. Walker liked it stowed aboard early."

"Did you tell Sergeant Howard about this?"

The young Negro shook his head. "I ain't seen him yet. Been sleeping. Only just heard about the accident half an hour ago. That's why I came in."

Manning turned slowly, found Seth standing at his shoulder. "You know what this means?"

Seth nodded soberly. "He'll have left the island by now, Harry. Probably all arranged beforehand."

Manning shook his head. "Never mind that. Get down to the harbour quick. See if you can find a boat that left last night, probably for Nassau. It shouldn't be too difficult. I'm going to see Viner. I'll meet you at the boat."

Seth trotted away and Manning turned back along the waterfront. The Old Ship was a couple of hundred yards

37

further on, not far from the jetty. As he approached, he saw Viner standing by the main gate.

The German spread his hands in a vague Continental gesture. "No luck, Harry. Bill Lumley hasn't taken on any new help since last season. All his present staff are islanders. Been with him for years."

"I've had a little more luck than that," Manning told him. "They missed someone off the passenger list. Man called Garcia. Apparently he never showed at flight time, but his luggage went aboard."

"Do you think he'll still be here?"

"Not a chance. I've sent Seth along the waterfront to see what he can find out."

At that moment there was a shout and they turned to see Seth running towards them. Sweat poured down the big Negro's face and his chest was heaving.

"You were right, Harry. Manny Johnson took someone over to Nassau and it sounds like our man. He was sitting in Flo's Bar around seven last night when this guy came in. Flo says they had a row. The trip had been fixed up two days before, but Manny wanted to call it off because of the weather. Flo says he only went because Garcia promised him another twenty quid."

Manning slapped him on the shoulder. "Good man. Go and cast off. We're getting out of here fast."

Seth ran along the jetty and Manning said to Viner, "You could still check on the other two hotels in case we're on a wild goose chase, but I don't think so."

He moved away and the German said sharply, "Be careful, Harry. These people play rough."

Manning turned, a slow, dangerous smile on his face like a fuse burning. "I only hope they do."

He ran along the jetty, jumped down to the deck and went into the wheelhouse as Seth cast off. He opened the throttle and as the *Grace Abounding* strained forward with a sudden surge, swung her out of harbour into the gulf.

5

Whistle Up the Duppies

They came into Nassau in the early afternoon. As the *Grace Abounding* skirted the green shoals of Athol Island, a great white liner moved out of the wide harbour, her rails lined with tourists taking a last look at New Providence.

The waterfront was crowded with work boats from the out-islands carrying everything from vegetables and fish to passengers and poultry. It was more like a market place than anything else and thronged with colourfully dressed Negroes talking endlessly amongst themselves, arguing good-humouredly as they bargained.

They tied up at an old jetty on the other side of the harbour and worked their way along Bay Street, looking for Manny Johnson's boat. They found it within half an hour and Manning dropped down to the deck and looked into the cabin. It was empty. As he climbed back onto the wharf, Seth turned from a couple of fishermen who sat on the wall baiting their lines.

"Seems Manny went on the town in a big way last night. Tossed his money around like it was going out of style."

"Probably flat on his back in some flea-pit sleeping it off," Manning said.

"Never knew him to save his money when he could be drinking. Maybe had his sleep and started all over again?"

"Could be. Start at the other end of Bay Street. I'll take this side. Try every joint you see. Somebody must know where he is." Manning glanced at his watch. "I'll meet you back here in a couple of hours."

Seth moved into the crowd at once and Manning started to work his way along the waterfront, calling in all the bars. He was wasting his time. Manny Johnson seemed to have covered most of them on the previous night, but no one had any idea where he was now.

It was just after four o'clock when he returned to the boat. He was hot and tired and there was a dull persistent ache somewhere at the back of his head. He lit a cigarette and leaned on the parapet, looking out over the harbour, wondering if Seth was having any better luck. After a while he turned to look along the waterfront and saw Morrison crossing the street towards him.

There was a wide grin on the American's face. "Say, I'd no idea you were coming over today."

"Didn't know myself," Manning said. "Something came up."

"Sorry about breaking our date this morning, but under the circumstances I didn't think you'd be interested. When Joe Howard said he was coming to Nassau I thought I'd go along for the ride. Never really had the chance to look the place over on my way in."

"It's quite a town," Manning said. "Plenty of night life and a first-rate casino."

"Sounds interesting." Morrison wiped sweat from his face with a handkerchief. "Too hot for comfort. What about a drink?"

Out of the corner of his eye Manning saw Seth emerge from the crowd and hesitate. "No thanks. Got some business to attend to. Maybe some other time."

He left the American standing there and joined Seth. "Any luck?"

The big Negro nodded. "Took some doing, but I finally made it. He's got a room in an hotel not far from here. What was Morrison after?"

"Wanted me to have a drink with him. I had to chop him off pretty short, but it can't be helped."

It took them about five minutes to reach their destination, a seedy tenement used as an hotel by seamen. It wasn't the sort of establishment that kept a receptionist. They entered a dark and gloomy hall and mounted a flight of wooden stairs. Seth opened a door at the far end of the corridor and led the way in.

The stench was appalling and Manning stumbled across to the window and opened the shutters. For several moments he stood there enjoying the cool breeze from the harbour and then he turned and looked down at Manny Johnson.

He lay on his back, mouth opened and twisted to one side, the soiled and filthy sheets half covering him and draping down to the floor. Manning sat on the edge of the bed, pulled him upright and slapped him gently across the face.

When the old man opened his eyes, he gazed at him with a peculiar fixed stare, and then something seemed to click and a slow smile appeared on his face.

"Harry Manning. What in hell are you doing here?"

"No time to explain that now, Manny. I want information and I want it fast." Manning gave him a cigarette and a light. "You ran someone over from Spanish Cay last night. A man called Garcia."

The old man rubbed a knuckle into his bloodshot eyes and nodded. "That's right. What do you want him for? He owe you money?"

Manning ignored the question. "Any idea where he went?"

"Search me. He paid up like a gent and hopped it."

"Did he take a cab?"

Manny shook his head. "He hired one of the kids who

bum around the wharf to carry his bag."

"Who was the kid?"

"You can't miss him. Hangs around the wharf all the time. Wears one of those American football jerseys some tourist gave him. Yellow thing with twenty-two in big black letters on the back. Reaches to his knees."

Manning turned enquiringly to Seth and the big Negro nodded. "I know the boy."

Manning got to his feet. "Thanks Manny. At least you've given us something to go on."

"My pleasure," the old man said. "Now if you'll kindly get to hell out of here, maybe I can get some sleep."

They found the boy sitting on the wharf, a few yards away from Manny's boat, with a fishing line, a small black dog curled up beside him. He was perhaps twelve years old and the yellow football jersey he wore contrasted vividly with his ebony skin.

Seth grinned down at him. "Doing any good?"

The boy shook his head. "They looking the other way. This ain't my lucky day."

"Maybe it could be." Manning produced a pound note and folded it between his fingers.

The boy's eyes went very round. "What you want, mister?"

"You know Mr. Johnson from Spanish Cay?"

The boy nodded. "That's his boat down there."

"He brought in a passenger last night," Manning said. "He hired you to carry his bag. I want to know where he went."

"For the pound?" Manning nodded and the boy grinned. "Mister, that's easy."

He handed his line and rod to another boy who sat on the edge of the wharf a few feet away. Then he got to his feet, nudged the dog with his toe and moved across Bay Street.

Manning and Seth found difficulty in keeping up with him as he trotted along the crowded pavement. He turned into a narrow alley and they followed him through a maze of back streets. Finally, he halted on the corner of a

42

small square that was entirely surrounded by dilapidated clapboard houses.

He pointed to one in the far corner. "That's it, mister. That's where he went. He paid me off in the back yard. I think he must have been Cuban. When the lady opened the door, she called him Juan."

Manning gave him the pound and the boy spat on it and grinned. "Anytime you want anything, just holler. I'm always down on the wharf there."

He whistled to his dog and ran back the way they had come.

Manning turned to Seth. "I want you to stay here. Give me ten minutes and then come looking."

The Negro frowned. "Maybe it's time we called in the police, Harry. Let them handle it."

Manning ignored him and moved across the square. The front door was boarded up and he followed a side passage that brought him into a back yard littered with empty tins and refuse of every description. He mounted four stone steps to the door and knocked.

Footsteps approached and it opened a few inches. A woman's voice said, "Who is it?"

"I'm looking for Juan," Manning said. "Juan Garcia. I'm an old friend of his."

There was the rattle of a chain and the door opened. "You'd better come in," she said and walked back along the corridor.

He closed the door and followed, wrinkling his nose at the stale smell compounded of cooking odours and urine. She opened a door, clicked on a light and led the way into a room. It was reasonably clean with a carpet on the floor and a double bed against the far wall.

She was a large, heavily built woman running dangerously to seed, the coffee-coloured skin and thick lips an indication of her mixed blood. She was still handsome in a bold, coarse sort of way and a sudden smile of interest appeared on her face.

"I'm Juan's girl—Hannah. Anything I can do?"

There was an unmistakable invitation in her voice and Manning grinned. "Not really."

"Is it business?"

"You could call it that."

"Well that's nice." She sat on the edge of the bed and smiled. "Give me a cigarette and tell me all about it."

She patted the bed beside her and Manning obliged. The gaudy housecoat she was wearing fell open when she crossed her knees revealing black stockings, the flesh bulging over the tops.

"I thought I knew most of Juan's friends. How come you've never been here before?"

"I move around a lot," Manning said. "Never in one place for long. Where did you say Juan had gone?"

She blew a cloud of smoke up towards the ceiling and leaned back against the pillow. "I didn't. As a matter of fact, he's been out of town for a couple of weeks. He only arrived back last night."

"What time did he go out this morning?"

"Around ten." She shrugged. "I went down to the market for food. When I returned, he'd gone. Left a message to say he'd be back this evening."

Manning shook his head. "I don't think so."

She frowned. "What are you trying to say, mister?"

"He's run out on you," Manning said.

She sat up, her eyes sparking angrily. "You don't know what you're talking about!"

"Where did he go?"

"He didn't say."

"But you've got a good idea?"

She stretched with a sigh of pleasure, arms extended, her breasts pushing hard against the thin material of her housecoat, and got to her feet. "Care for a drink?"

He nodded and she crossed to a cupboard, took out a bottle of gin and two glasses and filled them. She came back to the bed and give him one.

"He's been acting funny for about a month now. Kept hinting he had some big deal lined up that would put us on easy street for the rest of our lives, but he wouldn't tell me what it was all about."

"Did you ever find out?"

She drank some of her gin and shook her head. "No,

but I followed him a couple of times. He always went to the same place."

"And where was that?"

"Why should I tell you?"

He took out his wallet and produced a five pound note. She grabbed it quickly and pushed it down into the deep valley between her breasts, her face creasing into a smile.

"A fortune teller called Mother Diamond. Lives in a house in Grant Street down near the harbour."

"And you never found out why he went there?"

She shook her head. "I couldn't very well tell him I'd been following him. He'd have slit my ears."

Manning finished his gin and stood up. "Thanks for the drink, but I've got to be moving."

She leaned back against the pillows and gazed at him fixedly. "What's your hurry? Juan won't be back for a couple of hours."

"If I were you, I shouldn't bank on that," he said and closed the door gently as her mouth went slack with astonishment.

Dusk was beginning to fall as he went across the square. He turned into the side street and Seth moved out of a doorway.

"Do any good, Harry?"

Manning nodded. "I think so. Ever hear of a fortune teller called Mother Diamond?"

Seth glanced at him sharply. "Sure, everybody knows her. She mixed up in this?"

"I'm not sure, but it looks like it. Know where her place is?"

"Not far from the waterfront." Seth appeared to hesitate and went on, "She's bad trouble, that woman, Harry. Don't pay to meddle with her. Lots of people found that out."

Manning lit a cigarette and grinned. "Afraid she might put a hex on me?"

There was sweat on the big Negro's face and all at once, his eyes seemed very white. "They say she can whistle up the duppies, Harry. They say she can bring the drowned men out of the sea."

Manning was aware of a sudden irrational coldness as if somewhere, someone had walked over his grave, but he managed to force a smile.

"Let's go and find out."

It was almost dark when they reached Grant Street. The house was detached and surrounded by a six-foot board fence painted white. Manning opened the gate and they walked along a brick path and paused at the bottom of a flight of rickety wooden steps.

He turned to Seth. "You stay here and keep out of sight. If you hear a disturbance, kick in the door."

Seth merged into the darkness without a word and Manning mounted the steps and knocked on the door. After a few moments, steps shuffled along the corridor and he could see a shadowy figure through the cracked frosted glass window. The door clicked open and an old woman looked out at him.

A scarlet bandana was tied around her head like a turban and her wrinkled skin was the colour of leather, long jet ear-rings hanging on either side of her face. The eyes were the most disturbing feature, absolutely black and yet containing a weird luminosity.

"Mother Diamond?"

"What do you want?" Her voice was strangely lifeless.

"I wonder if you could spare me a few moments."

"You wish to consult the stars?"

"That's right. I was told you could help me."

She nodded at once. "Come in."

The hall was gloomy and filled with a smell of incense that caught at the back of the throat in a curiously unpleasant manner. She pulled back a heavy velvet drape and opened a door.

The room was sparsely furnished, the only light a single lamp on a small table. He took a chair and she sat opposite, several books at her elbow and a pad of blank paper in front of her.

"Give me the date of your birth, the place and time. The time is most important."

He told her and looked over her shoulder at the

shadows crawling out of the corners, pushing against the light thrown out by the lamp. He wondered what his next move should be, but decided to wait till she gave him an opening.

She consulted several books, making notes on the pad, and finally nodded. "Do you believe in the powers of the supernatural?"

"Would I be here if I didn't?"

"You are ambidextrous?"

For the moment, he was completely thrown off balance. "How in hell did you know that?"

"Many born under the sign of Scorpio are." She looked at the notes again. "Life for you is often a battleground."

"You can say that again."

She nodded calmly. "Mars, Sun and Neptune in conjunction on the mid-heaven will result in a certain sharpness of tongue and temper. You are often your own worst enemy."

In spite of himself, Manning laughed harshly. "I think that's bloody marvelous."

The old woman looked across, eyes glinting in the lamplight. "You find something humorous in what I say?"

"Something like that."

She carefully piled her books on top of each other. "Who did you say recommended you to come here?"

"I didn't," Manning said, "but since you ask, it was Juan Garcia."

Her eyes regarded him unwinkingly. "I know no one of that name."

"Well, how about taking a look into your crystal ball? You might see him skulking around in some dark corner."

"I think you'd better leave," she said calmly.

"You're making a big mistake."

A slight breeze touched the back of his neck and the door creaked. A voice said, "It is you who has made the mistake, Mr. Manning."

The man who advanced into the lamplight was wearing a white linen suit and his face was shaded by a Panama hat. The eyes were cold and hard and as full of menace as the .38 automatic in his right hand.

"Surprise, surprise," Manning said softly. "Juan Garcia, I presume?"

The other shook his head and for a brief moment, his teeth gleamed whitely. "I'm afraid not, señor. My name is Pelota. At this very moment, poor Juan is on the high seas bound for Cuba and what he fondly believes to be his just reward for his little exploit on Spanish Cay." He sighed heavily. "You have a saying in English. One get's one's reward in heaven."

"Is that where Garcia's going to get his?" Manning said.

Pelota shook his head. "He will not need to go that far, my friend. We have a little paradise here on earth called the Isle of Tears."

Mother Diamond cut in sharply. "Enough of this nonsense. This man is dangerous. I won't have him in my house. It was not in our agreement."

Pelota's eyes flickered towards her angrily and Manning seized the lamp from the table, pulled it from its socket and plunged the room into darkness. As he jumped for the shelter of a horse-hair sofa, Pelota fired twice, orange flame momentarily lighting the room.

Manning scrambled to one knee and Pelota cried, "Better come out, Manning. You haven't a chance."

At that moment, the door was kicked open, a great shaft of light flooding in from the corridor, picking Pelota out of the dark. He turned in alarm. As he started to raise his automatic, a bullet caught him in the centre of the forehead, lifting him back against the old woman.

As Manning got to his feet, the main light was switched on. Morrison was standing in the doorway, a revolver in one hand, Viner and Joe Howard at his shoulder.

6

The Man from C.I.A.

When Manning came out of the commissioner's office, he found Seth and Viner sitting on a bench in the waiting room. The Negro had a dressing taped to one side of his head and looked strained and ill.

He forced a smile. "Everything okay, Harry?"

Manning nodded. "How do you feel?"

"Not too good. Never even saw what hit me. Do you think they'll get anything out of him?"

"Pelota?" Manning shook his head. "The hospital rang through a few minutes ago. He's dead. The Commissioner and Morrison are discussing it now."

"I still haven't been able to work out where Morrison fits into all this," Viner said. "Who is he, anyway?"

"Central Intelligence Agency," Manning said. "Apparently they've been expecting trouble in these parts for some time. They sent him down here to see what he could turn up."

"I thought there was something special about him when I found him at police headquarters with Joe Howard." Viner grinned wryly. "Forgive me, Harry, but it seemed the sensible thing to do with you apparently running headlong into trouble. I hired a launch and followed you over."

"Good thing you did," Manning said. "That explains my meeting with Morrison on the wharf. Presumably you followed us."

Viner nodded. "All the way. We were in the garden at Mother Diamond's when the shooting started. That's when we broke in."

"Now she's a weird old bird if you like," Manning said. "Put a curse on me as they took her downstairs."

"Did they get anything out of her?"

"Not a thing. They only used her place as a clearing house. She was in it for the money, that's all."

At that moment, the door to the Commissioner's office opened and Morrison came out. He grinned. "I don't know about you guys, but I could use a drink."

"Good idea," Manning said.

They went out into the cool night and walked towards the waterfront. When they reached the corner of Bay Street, Seth caught hold of Manning's sleeve.

"If it's okay with you, I'll go back to the boat, Harry. I don't feel so good."

"You do that," Manning said. "Get some sleep. I'll be along later."

They watched him negotiate the busy street successfully, then walked along the pavement and entered the first bar they came to. It was still early by Nassavian standards and the place was almost deserted. Morrison ordered gin slings and they sat in a secluded booth in the corner.

"What happens now?" Manning said.

Morrison shrugged. "Looks like we've hit a brick wall. Pelota dead and our only lead on the way to the Isle of Tears, God help him."

"What is this place?" Manning asked.

"A small island off the Cuban coast about a hundred

and thirty miles south of Andros. There's a port there called San Juan. Used to be a centre for deep-sea fishermen. Since the revolution, they've been forbidden to come up to the islands any more. I hear the town is on the decline in a big way."

"Pelota seemed to think there was still something pretty special about the place."

"There is," Morrison said. "An old fortress they've turned into a prison for political offenders. It's the final resting place for anyone they really want to get rid of. So far nobody's survived long enough to be released."

"So that's what Pelota meant when he said Garcia would receive his reward here on earth."

Morrison nodded. "I don't know what the poor devil's expecting. If he's lucky, it'll be a bullet."

There was a short silence and then Viner said slowly, "Forgive me, Mr. Morrison, but it would appear that there is much more to this affair than appears on the surface. Am I right?"

Morrison took his time over a lighted cigarette. When he looked up, his face was grim. "By agreement with Great Britain, the United States has certain bases in the Bahamas."

"You mean in connection with the Canaveral project?"

Morrison nodded. "There are stations containing electronic brains which track, guide and probe missile behaviour during flights, on Grand Bahama, San Salvador and several other islands."

"Everyone knows that. It's common knowledge."

"Three weeks ago, one of them was badly sabotaged."

"You've kept damned quiet about it," Manning said.

"We had to. You can imagine the king-sized international row there'd be if it got out."

"And you think it was the same people who were responsible for this latest affair?" Viner said.

Morrison nodded. "We think they're based here in the Bahamas."

Manning whistled softly. "Seven hundred islands and two thousand cays and rocks. That's quite an area to search."

"And the whole thing's got to be done under cover. We just can't afford a stink at this stage. The eyes of the whole world are going to be turned this way when the President and your Prime Minister meet here in a couple of weeks."

"The Russians as usual, I suppose?" Viner said.

"I don't think so. Since the Cuban crisis, they've been leaning over backwards to keep things from boiling over. More likely some undercover group of Cuban fanatics. They're the only ones who'd stand to gain from promoting another international row. They haven't been too pleased with Moscow lately. Maybe they're trying to force their hand."

"And Garcia's the only lead you've got?" Viner said.

"And he'll be landing in San Juan about now."

Manning went to the bar and got himself a large rum. Whn he came back, he was frowning. "The word is, you've got agents all over Cuba. Why can't someone go to San Juan, see what he can dig up on Garcia. For all we know, he could be sitting in the best hotel in town living it up."

"Somehow I don't think so." Morrison shook his head.

"Surely it's worth checking on?"

"In any case, we've been having to take it pretty steady ourselves since the crisis. We don't want another storm at the moment any more than the Russians do. A Yank in Cuba just now would be like a red rag to a bull."

"How about an Englishman?"

Morrison frowned. "You must be crazy."

"I don't see why not," Manning said. "Relations between Cuba and Britain aren't exactly marvellous, but they're better than yours are."

"You'd be running your head straight into a noose."

Manning shrugged. "All I need is a good cover story."

"We couldn't help you. We couldn't help you at all. You'd be strictly on your own."

"Who said I needed any help? If I went, it would be for personal reasons. I've as much interest as you have in running this group down."

Morrison shook his head. "An attractive offer, Manning. I won't deny that, but it wouldn't work. In the first place, you just couldn't sail into San Juan. They'd clap you in gaol the moment you landed."

"I don't know about that," Viner said. "There are men from the islands, British citizens, who still make the occasional run to San Juan *and* out again."

Morrison turned to him and frowned. "Are you sure you know what you're talking about?"

Viner selected a cigarette and fitted it into his holder. "My business activities are varied, Mr. Morrison. They take me, on occasion, into strange places." He lit his cigarette and blew out a cloud of smoke. "On the southern tip of Andros Island there is a small fishing port called Harmon Springs. The people who live there are Greeks, mainly sponge fishermen from the Aegean who moved out here forty years ago. Deep-sea fishermen now. Some of them still make the run to San Juan with tuna and wahoo. The Cubans welcome them because supplies of big game fish are limited these days. The Greeks get a good price."

Morrison turned to Manning. "Did you know about this?"

Manning shook his head. "I've never been to Harmon Springs. They don't exactly encourage visitors. Still talk Greek amongst themselves and stick to the old customs. I can believe what Viner says. They're pretty tough customers. I can't think of much on top of the sea or below it that would frighten a Greek. They're the best divers in the world."

"How come you know so much about them?"

"I was in the Aegean for three years during the war with the Special Boat Service."

Morrison's face was pinched with excitement as he turned to Viner. "Got any contacts down there?"

Viner shook his head. "I'm afraid not. Most of what I've told you is hearsay. I can guarantee the information to be accurate, but that's all."

"It's good enough for me," Manning said flatly.

Morrison stared down into his glass for a moment or two. When he looked up, he had regained his composure. "I could let you have money. As much as you need, but that's all. If you go, you're strictly on your own. We know nothing about you."

Manning got to his feet and crossed to the window. Rain spattered against the glass and a small wind moved in from the sea, calling to him as it moaned through the rigging of the fishing boats moored to the wharf. A sudden shiver of excitement moved inside him. He smiled to himself, turned and went back to the table.

"If I'm going to get anywhere at Harmon Springs I'll need a good cover story. Let's have another drink and see what we can cook up."

7

Beware of Greeks

It was just before noon on the following day when the *Grace Abounding* came into Harmon Springs. Seth was at the wheel with old man Saunders acting as deck-hand and Manning stood at the rail wearing a panama hat and lightweight suit in tropical worsted.

As the boat rounded the curved promontory crowded with its white houses, a single-masted caique, sails belly-ing in the breeze, moved out to sea, passing so close that he could see the great eyes painted on each side of the prow to ward off evil spirits.

He raised his hand in greeting, but the man at the tiller ignored him completely and Saunders spat over the rail. "Nasty bastards they are down here, Harry. Half of them still build their boats to suit themselves."

The engines began to falter as they slowed to enter harbour. Several deep-sea launches were moored to the jetty, but on the white curve of sand, brightly painted caiques were beached and fishermen sat beside them mending their nets while naked children chased each other in the shallows.

It was like something from another world and by some trick of memory, Manning's mind went back through the years to the war and his time in the Aegean with the Special Boat Service.

He went into the cabin. A couple of cameras in leather cases were on the table and he slung them over his shoulder. He put on a pair of sun glasses, picked up a canvas grip and went up on deck.

They were already working alongside the wooden jetty. As he watched, the engine stopped, and everything seemed curiously still in the great heat. A couple of youths leaned against the rail smoking and three old men dozed in the sun, but no one made any attempt to catch the line that Saunders threw to them. He cursed and, stepping over the rail, picked up the line and ran it round a stanchion.

"Lousy bastards!" he muttered.

As Manning joined him, Seth moved out of the wheelhouse. "We'll hang around for an hour or two, Harry. Just to see what happens."

Manning shook his head. "I'll be in touch, Seth. Don't worry."

He stood there waiting and Seth sighed and went back into the wheelhouse. A moment later, the engines rumbled into life again. Saunders unlooped the line and stepped over the rail.

Manning waited until the *Grace Abounding* was passing out of harbour before picking up his canvas grip. The three old men were all sitting up straight eyeing him curiously and the two youths had stopped talking. He went past them, his footsteps booming hollowly on the wooden planking, and turned along the waterfront.

The little town seemed strangely still as if waiting for something to happen and, near at hand, someone started to sing. He followed the sound and came to a bar on the corner of a side street. Just inside the entrance, a youth sprawled in a chair against the wall and sang in a low

56

voice, his fingers gently stroking the strings of a *bouzouki*.

He made no effort to move. Manning stared down at him, anonymous in his dark glasses, and then stepped carefully over the outstretched legs and moved inside. The place was dark and cool with a marble-topped bar and three men sat at a small table drinking.

The man behind the bar was middle-aged, his wrinkled face the colour of mahogany, but his blue eyes were full of life and the mouth was shrewd and kindly. As Manning moved towards him, all conversation died.

He dropped his canvas grip and placed the cameras on the counter. "I could do with a drink. Something long and cool."

The man grinned, put a tall glass on the bar and spooned ice into it. "Journalist?"

Manning nodded. "I might be around here for a day or two. I could do with a room. Can you do anything for me?"

"Sure I can. It's nothing fancy, but the food's good."

The *bouzouki* player struck a single angry chord and the men at the table laughed. One of them called across to the youth in Greek. "Heh, Dimitri, don't you like the look of the fancy man? Maybe he'll beat your time with the girls. No more lolling on the beach after dark."

"Why don't you shut up?" the boy replied angrily.

They were typical rough seamen of a kind to be found the world over. Men who worked hard and played hard and didn't accept strangers easily. Manning turned, removed his sun glasses and looked at them calmly. The smiles faded a little and they leaned together, muttering in low voices.

As he turned back to his drink, one of them said loudly in Greek, "So Dimitri's just a bag of wind after all. A bag of wind dressed up in fancy clothes."

The youth jumped to his feet. For a moment, he seemed to hesitate and then moved along the bar, deliberately jogging Manning's elbow as he raised his glass to his mouth.

As the rum spilled across the bar, Manning put down

the glass and turned to face him. "Now you can buy me another one."

"Buy your own," the boy said.

Manning slapped him back-handed across the face, sending him staggering against the wall. "I shan't ask you again."

The boy's hand moved to his hip-pocket. As he flung himself forward, a six-inch blade honed like a razor seemed to jump out of his right fist. Manning stepped quickly to one side. He grabbed for the wrist and twisted it round and up into the small of the boy's back so that he screamed and dropped the knife. Almost in the same motion, Manning pushed him across the table, scattering the three occupants and their drinks.

"Never send a boy to do a man's work," he said in Greek.

There was a moment of stunned silence. As they started to rise, the barman moved round the counter fast, a wooden truncheon in one hand. "The first one to start, gets his skull cracked. You men tried to have a little fun, but you made a mistake. Let that be an end to it."

They resumed their seats and the boy turned and ran from the entrance. The barman smiled up at Manning and held out his hand. "Nikoli Aleko. You speak good Greek for an Englishman."

"Spent three years in the Aegean during the war, but that was a long time ago. Manning's the name. Harry Manning."

"Another drink, Mr. Manning? On the house."

"On me," Manning said. "For all of us." He pulled forward a chair and sat down and the three men grinned.

"Anyone who can speak Greek as good as you is okay with me," one of them said. "Have a cigarette."

Aleko brought the drinks and they solemnly toasted each other. As Manning put down his glass, one of them said, "You here for the fishing?"

"I'm a photographer. A big American magazine's just commissioned me to do a feature for them."

"On Harmon Springs?"

Manning shook his head. "On Cuba. They want me to

go to a place called San Juan. Take a few pictures. See how things have altered since the revolution."

They looked at each other in surprise and then one of them raised his glass. "Good luck, my friend. You're going to need it."

"Any special reason?"

"Nobody goes to San Juan these days. It's the last place God made."

"I was told differently in Nassau. I heard that boats from here often made the trip."

"That was last year. Things have changed plenty since then."

Manning took out his wallet. "I'm on a pretty good expense account. I'd pay well."

The man who had been doing most of the talking laughed harshly. "My friend, we have a saying. If you want a man to risk his life for money, look for a poor man."

The other two laughed uproariously and one of them said, "He should try Papa Melos. The state he's in, he'd do anything."

Manning got to his feet and moved across to the bar. "Did you hear that?"

Aleko nodded. "They're right in what they say. Before the crisis, many of our boats called at San Juan with tuna. The Cubans are forbidden to come north so the prices were high. Since the crisis, everything's changed."

"You mean the Cubans have forbidden them to call?"

Aleko shook his head. "Not exactly, but the atmosphere's bad. One can't tell which way they will jump. Nobody wants to lose his boat."

"Who's this Papa Melos they mentioned?"

Aleko smiled. "A wonderful old man. He runs a motor cruiser, the *Cretan Lover*. His only boy, Yanni, was drowned last year. He has a daughter, Anna, a bright girl. He sent her to America to be educated. A place called Vassar. Maybe you heard of it?"

Manning grinned. "I've heard of it all right."

"He squeezed himself dry to keep her there and after the boy was killed, he had difficulty in getting good

59

catches. The girl turned up three months ago. When she found out what had happened, she refused to go back. She's been crewing for him ever since."

"What do they go after—tuna?"

Aleko shook his head. "Not any more. There's a reef about ten miles west near Blair Cay. The old man found mother of pearl there. He's been diving for it lately."

"At his age?" Manning said incredulously. "How deep?"

"Fifteen, maybe twenty fathoms, and the suit he's using must be all of forty years old."

"He must be crazy."

"He doesn't want to lose his boat, that's all. That and Anna are the only two things he's got left in the world."

"Do you think he'd be interested in running me across to San Juan?"

Aleko shrugged. "A desperate man is capable of anything."

"You never said a truer word." Manning picked up his grip and the cameras. "I'll have a look at that room now, if you don't mind."

As he followed Aleko along a whitewashed corridor, a sudden spark of excitement moved inside him as he realized, with complete certainty, that he had found the solution to his problem.

Aleko was the owner of a small twelve-foot launch which he was willing to hire out. Two hours later after a change of clothes and one of the best meals he'd had in a long time, Manning took her out of harbour and turned west along the southern tip of the island.

The sea was like glass and the cloudless blue sky dipped away to the horizon. He lit a cigarette and sat back in the swing chair, one hand on the wheel, wondering about Papa Melos. What made a man keep on fighting when every card in the deck was stacked against him? There was no answer. Some men went under struggling to the last. Others sank without a cry.

He rounded Blair Cay within forty minutes and saw the boat anchored about a quarter of a mile out in the gulf. He slowed down and coasted in towards her, aware of the dull rhythmic throbbing of the mechanical pump that forced air down through the blue water to the man below.

It was difficult to believe that anyone could still use the old-fashioned canvas suit with all the paraphernalia of air and lifelines in this era of the frogman with his compressed air cylinders. The aqualung was superior in every way and with it, the diver became a completely free agent.

He could see the girl as he drew nearer, rather small in a bright red shirt and canvas jeans, long hair twisted into a pigtail at the back. She was turning the handle of the life-line crank, hauling her father in, and seemed completely unaware of Manning's approach.

Quite suddenly, the crank stopped revolving. She tugged at the handle, exerting all her strength and then went to the rail and looked over. She ran back to the crank and swung all her weight against the handle with no result. The next moment, she turned and dived over the rail.

Manning cut the engine and drifted alongside. He fastened the line quickly, ran across to the crank and threw all his strength against the handle. It refused to budge. As he moved back to the rail, the girl surfaced beside the wooden ladder gasping for breath. Somehow, her pigtail had come undone and long, blue-black hair floated around her in the water. He reached down and pulled her over the rail.

"What's wrong down there?"

She was completely distraught. "I couldn't reach him! I couldn't reach him!"

"How deep is he?"

"Ten fathoms, maybe more. I've got to try again."

She scrambled to her feet, turning to the rail. At that moment, a great gout of air erupted to the surface. Manning sat down and pulled off his shoes and jacket.

"You stay with that crank. The line's probably snagged on a niggerhead. The moment I signal, start pulling him in."

He scrambled onto the roof of the wheelhouse, poised

61

on the edge for several seconds, forcing as much oxygen as possible into his lungs, and dived.

Once in the Caymans, he had free-dived just over a hundred feet, but that had been ten years before. Ten years of hard living. Of going downhill in every way.

As a diver descends, the deepening layer of water filters the sunlight, absorbing all red and orange rays. At fifty feet, as he descended the face of the great cliff, Manning found himself swimming into a neutral zone. Visibility was still excellent, but all colours were muted and autumnal.

At sixty feet the line had looped itself around a gnarled spike of coral, tightening into a crevasse. He freed it quickly and moved on.

He found the old man on a wide ledge on the face of the cliff. The ancient canvas suit had been slashed open against the razor-sharp coral as he had struggled to free himself. Water had forced its way into the suit and only the continuing pressure of fresh air being pumped into the great bronze helmet kept it at chest level.

Manning, his vision completely distorted, had a brief glimpse of the face peering out at him before he pulled hard on the lifeline, his agreed signal with the girl. He started upwards, dragging the old man behind him.

The pressure in his ears was fantastic and bells seemed to be tolling melodiously somewhere near at hand. great waves of sound beating against him.

Far above, he could see the silhouette of the *Cretan Lover*'s hull and he released his hold on the old man and spiralled upwards in a cloud of champagne bubbles.

He broke surface beside the ladder and hung there for a moment, gasping for breath. When he pulled himself over the rail, the girl was turning the handle for dear life, sweat pouring down her face.

"He's coming," she cried. "He's coming."

Manning was conscious of the pains in his limbs, of the gigantic hand that pressed against his chest. He fought against the darkness that moved in on him and heaved on the line with all his strength.

The old man broke through to the surface beside the

ladder. Manning and the girl heaved together and he staggered over the rail and collapsed on deck.

Manning watched as the girl unscrewed the bronze wingnuts and then his vision blurred and the sound of her voice seemed to come from the other end of a tunnel. When he went, he seemed to dive head-first into dark waters.

8

The Cretan Lover

As Manning emptied the cup, Anna Melos filled it again. The coffee was so hot that it scalded the back of his throat. As it burned its way into his stomach, he felt life returning.

She went into the galley and he watched her over the rim of the cup. Her slim, almost boyish figure seemed strangely sexless and yet the lips had an extra fullness that suggested sensuality.

Turning, she caught him watching her and smiled. "Feeling better?"

He nodded. "No time to decompress, that was the trouble. It doesn't do any real harm if it's only once in a while."

"But not too often," she said. "When I was twelve, I saw my uncle Alexias die of the bends. It wasn't pretty."

A step sounded on the companionway and her father

came in. He was about seventy with grizzled hair and a white moustache that stood out clearly against the swarthy skin.

He sat down and started to fill an ancient briar pipe. "How do you feel?"

"I think I'll survive."

"That was quite something. I must have been a good seventy feet down. Not many men can free dive that far."

"Oh, I've met a few," Manning said. "Down in the Caymans, they go to a hundred and fifty, but they use a lead weight to get there quickly."

"You done much diving before? Real diving, I mean."

"With an aqualung. You wouldn't get me into the sort of contraption you were wearing." Manning grinned. "The only good thing that comes out of this is the fact that you've ruined it."

"The suit?" Papa Melos shrugged. "I can patch it up easily."

Anna had been cutting sandwiches in the galley and now she came forward quickly. "No, papa. Never again."

"You would prefer Mikali to take the boat?" He took her hand in his. "We must live, Anna. What else can I do?"

She turned away quickly and he smiled at Manning, changing the subject deliberately. "Good thing you came by when you did."

"It was no accident," Manning said. "I'm looking for someone to run me down to San Juan. Nikoli Aleko told me you might be interested."

"San Juan, on the Isle of Tears?" The old man frowned. "What would you want to go there for?"

"I'm a free-lance photographer. I'm doing a Cuban feature for an American magazine. I was told boats from Harmon Springs sometimes put in at San Juan with tuna. I served in the Aegean during the war so I speak a little Greek. I thought maybe I could be passed off as a crew member."

"Sure, I used to make the trip. We all did. They paid top price for tuna down there, but things have changed since the crisis. You can't tell which way those people might jump; could even impound my boat." Papa Melos shook his head. "I'd like to help you, Mr. Manning, but not this time."

Manning reached for his jacket and took out his wallet. He opened it and produced a wad of banknotes. "Five hundred dollars—a thousand. Name your own price."

The girl's breath hissed sharply between her teeth. "Papa, with money like that you could pay Mikali what we owe him. Our worries would be over."

The old man stared down at the money as if hypnotized and then shook his head slowly. "If I go to San Juan, I'd probably lose the boat anyway. At least I've got till the end of the month to pay Mikali what I owe him."

Manning schooled his face to a pleasant smile. "Not to worry. There must be somebody in Harmon Springs who wants to earn that kind of money."

He was up on deck and stood at the rail, looking out towards the island, wondering what the hell he was going to do next. A moment later, the girl joined him.

"I'm sorry," she said. "I feel that we owe you so much, but the boat is my father's whole life. He couldn't stand the thought of losing her."

"Do you really think he can raise the money to pay off this man Mikali?" Manning said.

She shook her head and turned to the rail, her slim shoulders hunched in defeat. For a brief moment he was conscious of an irrational tenderness. It was as if she were a young child faced with something she couldn't handle, that he must comfort at all costs.

He became aware of the sound of an engine and a speedboat roared round the tip of Blair Cay and come towards them. The girl raised her head, looked at it for a moment, then hurried below.

When she returned, her father was with her. He leaned against the rail, a frown on his face. "Looks like Mikali's boat. I wonder what he wants?"

The speedboat was being driven by Dimitri, the youth Manning had handled so roughly at the bar. Mikali was a large thick-set individual. In his day, he must have been a powerful man, but now he was running to fat and the armpits of his linen jacket were badly stained with sweat. He clambered up the ladder and Dimitri stayed at the wheel.

"And what the hell do you want?" Papa Melos said in Greek.

Mikali wiped his balding head with a handkerchief. "Don't take that tone with me, you old vulture. Three days I've been trying to catch you. Always, you stay out of my way."

"I've got nothing to say to you. Not till the end of the month."

"Now that's where you're wrong," Mikali said. "The extension I gave you was purely out of the goodness of my heart." He glanced at Anna. "I'd hopes that we might have been able to come to a sensible arrangement about things in general, but that doesn't seem to have worked out."

The old man flushed angrily. "Say what you have to say and get off my boat."

"*My* boat, you mean." Mikali produced a document and held it out. "This is a writ of attachment. You've got until noon on Friday to pay me my money. Twelve hundred dollars."

The old man gave a roar of anger. He tore the writ from Mikali's hand and swung hard with his right fist. The years were against him. Mikali blocked the punch with ease, grabbed him by the shirt-front and slapped him heavily across the face.

The girl screamed and ran forward, tearing at him with her fingers. He pushed her away with such force that she staggered across the deck and lost her balance. As he raised his hand to strike the old man again, Manning grabbed him by the shoulder and swung him round so that they faced each other.

"How about trying me?" he said. "I'm a bit nearer your size."

Mikali opened his mouth to speak and Manning smashed a fist into it. As he staggered backwards, Manning hit him again, the force of the blow lifting him over the rail. The Greek hit the water with a tremendous splash

67

and went under. He came up a couple of feet away from the speedboat and Dimitri grabbed him by the collar and tried to haul him over the stern.

Manning went down the ladder quickly, jumped into the speedboat and helped him. Mikali sprawled across the rear seat, his clothes clinging to his gross body, blood trickling from his smashed mouth. Manning produced his wallet and counted out twelve one hundred dollar bills. He stuffed them into the Greek's breast pocket.

"All debts paid, Mikali. Bother the old man again and I'll break your neck." He turned to Dimitri. "And you're a witness. He's had his money. Don't forget."

He jumped for the ladder and Dimitri started the engine and took the speedboat away in a long sweeping curve. Manning watched until it had disappeared behind the cay and then turned.

The old man was sitting on the bench outside the wheelhouse, filling his pipe. When it was going to his satisfaction, he puffed out a cloud of smoke and shrugged. "So we go to San Juan?"

"You sure?" Manning said.

Papa Melos nodded. "What else can I do? You save my life, you save my boat. It's fate."

"What about you?" Manning said to the girl.

She was standing at the other rail, her back towards him. She turned and looked at him gravely. "I don't see that we really have any choice. We are a proud people, Mr. Manning. We like to pay our debts."

For a moment, Manning had an insane desire to tell them the truth, to warn them that they were imperilling much more than the boat if they went through with this thing. But then he remembered his reason for going.

He shrugged. "That's fine by me. I'm ready to start when you are."

9

South from Andros

He was not conscious of having slept, only of being awake and looking at his watch and realizing, with a sense of shock, that it was three in the morning. He pulled on his heavy reefer jacket and left the cabin.

There was a slight sea mist lifting off the water and the *Cretan Lover* was kicking along at a tremendous pace. There was no moon, but the night sky was a jewel-studded delight and there was a strange luminosity to the water. He walked along the heaving deck, stepping over the three tuna they had caught on the previous afternoon, and went into the wheelhouse.

Papa Melos was standing at the wheel. He cut a fine, weird figure, his head apparently disembodied in the light from the compass.

"How are things going?" Manning said.

"Couldn't be better."

He slipped to one side, allowing Manning to take over the wheel, and leaned against the door filling his pipe.

"What time will we make San Juan?"

The old man shrugged. "If the weather holds, just before noon tomorrow."

"Will there be any restriction on how long we can stay?"

"There never used to be, but as I said before, things have changed."

"Will we have much trouble finding a buyer for the fish?"

"I shouldn't think so, not with tuna as prime as those are." Papa Melos applied a match to the bowl of his pipe. "You're a handy man with a rod. As good as any I've seen. Come to think of it, for a photographer, you're a pretty good sailor."

"I've been around small craft all of my life and the Special Boat Service was a first-rate grounding."

"But that was a long time ago," Papa Melos said. Before the flood."

There was a question in his voice, unspoken but still there. Manning ignored it and said easily, "Some things a man never forgets how to do."

"I suppose not." The old man yawned. "Think I'll get some sleep. I'll take over at seven."

He moved away along the deck, humming to himself, and Manning lit a cigarette, pulled a hinged seat down from the wall and settled back comfortably, the wheel steady in his hands.

There was little point in worrying what might happen when they reached San Juan. He would have to play the cards as they fell. A slight, ironic quirk tugged at the corners of his mouth. Come to think of it, he seemed to have been doing just that for the greater part of his life.

Gradually his mind wandered back along forgotten paths and he thought of people and incidents long gone. This was a period he looked forward to at sea. To be alone with the night and the boat. It was if the world had ceased to exist.

The door opened softly, coinciding with a spatter of rain against the windows. He smelt the aroma of coffee heavy on the morning air and there was another, more subtle fragrance.

"What's wrong with bed at this time in the morning?" he said.

"The best part of the day," she told him and pulled down another seat.

She handed him a mug of coffee and a sandwich and they ate in companionable silence, their knees touching. Afterwards, he gave her a cigarette and they sat there smoking as rain hammered forcefully against the window.

"You love the sea, don't you?" she said suddenly.

"I suppose I do," he said, momentarily off guard. "It's rather like a woman—capricious and not very reliable, but that doesn't mean you love her the less."

She smiled. "You're the strangest photographer I've ever met."

As with her father, there was an unspoken question in her voice and he suddenly knew he was on dangerous ground.

"I had a salvage business in Havana with a side-line in underwater photography. When the revolution came, I hung on till the last minute like a hell of a lot of other people who didn't see which way the wind was blowing. Only got out by the skin of my teeth. Lost everything."

He was unable to keep the bitterness out of his voice and she leaned across impulsively and put a hand on his arm. When she spoke, her voice was warm and full of sympathy. "I'm sorry."

"No need to be. I was luckier than most of the poor devils who hang around Miami waiting for something unpleasant to happen to Castro. I knew the right people and that always helps. I've managed to make a steady living at this free-lance game."

"This trip to San Juan? It means a lot to you?"

"More than anything else in the world right now," he said flatly.

"Then I'm glad we agreed to go."

Suddenly, he was ashamed of the lies and the deceit, of the fact that he was running this girl and her father headlong into danger, mixing them up in a situation that

71

had nothing to do with them. For a moment, he was filled with an overwhelming desire to tell her everything, but she forestalled him.

"There's nothing quite like it, is there? A small boat and the sea on a night like this. All one's real troubles suddenly seem unimportant."

Her face was faintly illuminated by the compass light, the eyes dark shadows that somehow gave her a strange, mysterious quality that was quite unique.

"You're a funny girl," he said. "Nikoli Aleko told me you were at Vassar?"

She nodded. "Until a few months ago. It was my father's idea. He'd been left a legacy. Like most Greeks, he believes there's nothing like an education so he decided to send me to the States. Only the best was good enough."

"What did you intend to do?"

"I was supposed to go to Oxford this year. I was hoping to read law."

"And now this."

"My brother Yanni was drowned last year. When papa wrote to tell me, he said there was no point in my coming home. That it was all over and done with."

"So you stayed?"

"There didn't seem any reason not to. In his letters, he said everything was fine."

"And you finally came home and found out different?"

"Something like that." She leaned forward, pressing her head against the window and stared out into the night. "You wouldn't understand this, but I didn't find my father. I found an old, beaten man travelling fast downhill, and he'd never seemed old to me before." She sighed. "He'd even had to borrow money on the boat to keep me at college. Apparently the legacy had run out even before Yanni died."

"And he thought he could make ends meet by going back to diving?"

"For desperate men there are only desperate remedies." She used almost the same words Aleko had used. "Of course, there was always Mikali's solution."

"You can't be serious?"

72

She shrugged. "We are a stubborn people, we stick to the old ways. Arranged marriages are still common amongst us. It was my father who refused permission."

"I should damn well think so." Manning was conscious of a sudden irrational anger. "There must be a better solution than that."

"But there is," she said, "and you have offered it to us."

There was nothing he could say and they sat there in silence and gradually, the rain stopped and dawn began to seep into the sky. Daylight came with a slight mist on the sea and a chill wind, but Manning hardly noticed.

Anna leaned back in the corner half asleep, all tiredness and strain wiped from her face. He sat there quietly watching her for a while and realized, with a sense of wonder, that she was beautiful. It was as if he had never really seen her before.

She opened her eyes and looked at him and a smile appeared on her face.

"Good morning, Harry," she said.

He smiled back, absurdly pleased she had used his first name. "A long night."

"I'd better get breakfast ready." She picked up the tray, moved to the door and hesitated. "This may be the last chance I have to speak for you on your own."

He waited, his heart a stone inside him. "Whatever happens in San Juan, you've given us hope. For that, I'll always be grateful."

And then she was gone and he sat there watching the door swing to and fro, listening to her footsteps fade away along the deck. When he opened a window to let in the cold air, his hands were trembling.

10

Isle of Tears

San Juan slumbered in the noonday heat as they turned past the concrete pill box on the point and moved into the narrow channel. On the far side, the cliffs lifted a hundred feet out of the water with an old Spanish fortress perched on top.

Papa Melos leaned out the wheelhouse window and nodded towards it. "They're using it as a prison for political offenders. I've heard some terrible stories about what goes on up there."

"I can believe them."

Manning looked up at the fortress. It was at least four hundred years old and the amenities had probably altered little since it was built. From the Inquisition to Castro. He sighed and shook his head. Time was a circle turning endlessly on itself. There was no beginning, no end.

San Juan itself was a typical small Cuban fishing port,

but there were few boats in the harbour and a strange air of decay hung over everything. Even the Cuban flag over the Town Hall hung like a limp rag in the great heat.

Papa Melos cut the engines and signalled to Manning to let go the anchor. For a moment longer, the *Cretan Lover* glided forward and then, with a gentle tug, it came to a halt fifty or sixty yards from the crumbling stone jetty that formed the south side of the harbour.

The old man stepped out of the wheelhouse and joined Manning at the rail. "We have to wait here till we've been cleared by the harbour-master."

Anna came out of the cabin. A blue silk scarf was bound about her head peasant-fashion and sun-glasses shaded her eyes. She moved beside him, her arms touching his.

"What do you think, Harry?" she said anxiously.

He tried to sound reassuring. "There's nothing to worry about. Everything's going to be fine."

Inside his shirt, tucked into his waistband, was a .38 calibre automatic and he touched the butt quickly to re-assure himself.

As they looked across the harbour a small rowing boat appeared from between two moored fishing-boats. The man at the oars was being urged on by a fat, bearded official in a crumpled khaki uniform.

Papa Melos gave an exclamation of relief. "It's still the same harbour-master, thank God. Luis Rafael is his name and he's as genial as he is fat."

"That could be important," Manning said.

As the boat bumped against the side of the launch, Rafael smiled up at them, his face shiny with sweat. He spoke English with a pronounced American accent.

"Papa Melos, by all that's holy. I thought it was your boat, but I couldn't believe my eyes. Long time no see."

Papa Melos leaned over the rail and they touched hands. "Luis, my old friend, good to see you." He waved towards Anna. "My daughter. You've heard me speak of her often."

Rafael positively beamed. "My pleasure, señorita." He turned again to the old man. "And how is Yanni?"

"Drowned in a bad storm off Andros six months ago," the old man said calmly and nodded towards Manning. "That is why I have Alexias here."

Rafael looked genuinely distressed and crossed himself quickly. "May he rest in peace."

"Are you coming aboard?"

The Cuban shook his head. "Bring her straight in to the jetty. I will meet you there. The occasion would seem to call for a drink."

"Is Bayo still running the hotel?"

Rafael nodded. "Trade isn't what it was, but he seems to manage. These are difficult times."

"For all of us," Papa Melos said. "We'll see you on the wharf."

Rafael gave a quick order to the oarsman who immediately started to row away and Papa Melos turned to Manning with a smile. "I think it's going to be all right."

"It certainly looks like it," Manning said. "What about this man Bayo you mentioned? Can he be trusted?"

The old man nodded. "These people are too Catholic ever to go Communist. That's where Castro is making his big mistake. There are a lot of people in Cuba like Luis Rafael and Bayo. Ordinary men who have to accept what happens because they've got to keep on living. Because they've got wives and families. That doesn't mean they have to like it. Castro will find that out to his cost one fine day."

He went back to the wheelhouse and started the engine as Manning cranked in the anchor. He moved to the prow and got ready with the line. Rafael was already on the jetty and as they coasted in, he spoke to a couple of loafers who moved forward. Manning tossed them the line and as they ran it round a stanchion, Papa Melos killed the engine.

The jetty was only a couple of feet above the rail and Manning climbed up, pulling Anna behind him. Rafael removed his cap and kissed her hand.

"A great pleasure. I have known your father for many years now." He looked down at the tuna and sighed heavily. "A long time since we've seen such beauties landed here. You'll have no trouble in selling them."

"That's what I hoped," Papa Melos said and they all walked along the jetty together.

"But why the long absence?" Rafael said. "It must be at least six months since a boat called here from Harmon Springs."

"To be honest, we weren't sure we'd be welcomed," Papa Melos told him. "Let's face it, things haven't been quite the same since the crisis."

"But we know our friends," Rafael said. "There is a large difference between Greeks from Harmon Springs and Yankee spies from Miami. Give us credit for that much sense."

"Well, it's nice to hear that. Perhaps when the others know how we've got on, they'll start coming again themselves."

"Nothing I'd like better."

The sign outside Bayo's place said: *Hotel*, and was as dilapidated as the rest of the waterfront. There were several wooden tables outside, but no customers, and Manning guessed that the place would probably liven up in the evening.

It was cool and dark inside and reasonably clean, with whitewashed walls and rush mats on the floor. There were more tables and chairs and a marble-topped bar in one corner, bottles ranged behind it on wooden shelves.

The man who leaned on the bar reading a newspaper was small and wiry. The right side of his face was disfigured by an ugly scar and the eye was covered by a black patch.

"Heh, Bayo, see who's here!" Rafael called.

Bayo glanced up in surprise. When he saw Papa Melos a delighted smile appeared on his face. He dropped the newspaper and came round the end of the bar.

"Papa Melos," he said in English, pumping the old man's hand. "A sight for sore eyes."

Papa Melos put a hand on the little Cuban's shoulder and frowned. "Your face, Bayo, what happened?"

Bayo shrugged, his smile slipping a little. "Nothing, my

friend. An accident three months ago. You have brought fish in?"

The old man nodded. "Three tuna."

"He needed the excuse to see how we were getting on," Rafael put in.

They all smiled and Papa Melos introduced Anna and Manning. "My daughter and Alexias Stavrou. He's crewing for me now."

"And Yanni? How is Yanni?"

"Drowned six months ago," Papa Melos said calmly.

A spasm of pain crossed the little Cuban's face and he reached instinctively to touch the old man's sleeve. "He was a good boy."

"None better," Papa Melos said. "It is God's will."

The slight awkward silence was quickly glossed over by Rafael who dropped his hat onto a table and pulled forward a chair for Anna. "But this is the time for wine, not talk. A bottle of your best is indicated, Bayo."

Bayo nodded eagerly. "I have some Chablis '57 cooling in the ice-box for Colonel Rojas, but he won't be in until this evening."

He disappeared into the back room and Manning turned to Rafael. "Who's this Colonel Rojas he mentioned?"

Rafael immediately looked uncomfortable. "He commands the fortress here. They have turned it into a prison for political offenders. Since the Bay of Pigs affair, it's had plenty of occupants."

"What is he? Police or army?"

The glance the Cuban threw over his shoulder before leaning forward was almost a reflex action. "They say he is of the D.I.E.R., señor. The military secret police. In Cuba today they have more power than anyone."

"What happened to Bayo?" Papa Melos said as he tapped tobacco into the bowl of his pipe. "His face is certainly one hell of a mess."

"Three months ago a new batch of prisoners was delivered to the fortress from the main island. Their guards were a rough lot. Real *barbudos* of the kind who were in the hills with the President. They got drunk and started to break the place up. When Bayo tried to stop them,

78

one of them slashed him across the face. He lost an eye."

"Nice people," Manning said.

Rafael shrugged. "In Cuba today, it is not wise to pass judgment on anything, señor. You would do well to remember that."

"I suppose you're right." Manning offered him a cigarette. "Is this the only hotel in town?"

"There was another, but it closed last month. No one comes for the fishing any more."

"Anyone staying here now?"

Rafael smiled. "I don't think Bayo has had a guest in six months. There will be plenty of room for you to stay, if that's what's worrying you."

At that moment, Bayo appeared from the rear, a clean white cloth over one arm and carrying a tray on which stood the bottle of wine and five glasses.

He put down the tray and lifted the bottle. "Nectar of the gods. See how the moisture has frozen on the outside."

"Perfect, my dear Bayo. Perfect. You must have known I was coming."

The man spoke in excellent English and completely filled the doorway. His face was shaded by a Panama hat and a soiled white linen suit draped loosely from the immense shoulders, only half-concealing the grotesque figure.

He carried a malacca cane in one hand and as he moved into the room, a look of complete terror appeared on Bayo's face and the bottle slipped between his nerveless fingers. Manning caught it neatly and placed it on the table.

"My thanks, señor," the fat man said. "A pity to waste good wine. But there are only five glasses here, Bayo."

As Bayo moved away quickly, Rafael jumped up, his face quite pale. "A chair, colonel."

"Thank you, my friend."

He flopped down with a groan. "The English have a saying. Only mad dogs and themselves go out in the midday sun. It would appear to me that there is much truth in this. Would you not agree?"

"The perfect remedy." Manning poured some wine into one of the glasses and pushed it across.

79

"My thanks, señor, but it would hardly be good manners for me to drink alone. Rafael, introduce me to your friends."

"But of course, Colonel Rojas."

So this was Rojas? Rafael babbled the introductions and Manning schooled his face to steadiness and poured wine into the glasses as Bayo returned.

Sweat stained the colonel's jacket in great patches and trickled along the folds of his fat face. He produced a red silk handkerchief, mopped the worst of it away and removed his panama. His head was quite bald and what little hair remained had been razored clean. But it was the eyes that were his most compelling feature, constantly in motion, cold and hard and utterly without mercy.

"Poor Bayo. I startled you, eh? I made you jump?" A muscle twitched in Bayo's face and Rojas laughed harshly, his body shaking like a jelly. "He hasn't been the same since his little accident last summer."

Anna leaned forward, anger sparkling in her eyes and Manning put a hand on her arm and reached for the bottle. "More wine, colonel?"

Rojas raised the glass to his lips and sighed with pleasure. "Exquisite! Such a delightful bouquet!" He put the glass down and produced a long Havana cigar from his breast pocket. "I hear you've brought tuna with you, captain."

Papa Melos nodded. "That was the purpose of the trip. Boats from Harmon Springs called here frequently, but that was before the crisis. I thought I'd see if we were still welcome."

Rojas turned to him in what appeared to be quite genuine amazement. "But our quarrel is not with your people, my friend. It is with the Americans and those who would help them."

There was a slight, awkward silence and Manning said calmly, "Well, that's certainly nice to know."

Rojas put a match to his cigar and puffed out a cloud of blue smoke. "So, the tuna were your only reason for calling here?"

The old man moistened dry lips. "But of course," he said, a ghastly smile on his face.

"Strange," Rojas said calmly, "I thought that perhaps Señor Manning here had intended taking a few photographs."

As a dry sob erupted from the old man's throat, Manning's hand slid inside his shirt, reaching for the butt of the automatic.

Rojas shook his head. "I don't think that would be very wise."

Something hard and cold nudged Manning in the side of the head and he turned and stared into the business end of a sub-machine-gun. The man who held it looked extremely competent. He wore a neat khaki uniform, a black beret and beard to match.

Manning put his hands on the table and the soldier reached inside his shirt and removed the automatic. Rojas poured himself another glass of wine and sipped it in leisurely fashion.

"You know, this is really quite excellent. The best year since the war. Bayo puts some on ice for me each day."

"I shouldn't have thought you were capable of telling the difference," Manning said.

For a moment, something flickered in the fat man's eyes and there was a curious quality of stillness about his whole body, and then he started to laugh, head thrown back, the flesh dancing across his great frame. When he finally gained control, there were tears in his eyes.

"My dear Señor Manning," he said, wiping them away with his silk handkerchief. "You know, I really think I'm going to enjoy you."

11

The Man in the Vaults

As the jeep pulled out of the ravine, Manning got his first full view of the fortress. It was perched spectacularly on the edge of a small plateau which jutted from the side of the mountain like a shelf. Beyond it, there were only the cliffs dropping a hundred feet into the sea.

He was in the rear seat, an armed soldier on either side of him, and Rojas sat up front with the driver. The walls of the ancient fortress were pierced for cannon and the gates stood open. They slowed for the sentry to raise a long wooden swing bar and Rojas turned and smiled.

"Spectacular, is it not, Señor Manning?"

Manning looked up at the great archway and the grim towers beyond. "All it needs are a couple of heads on spikes over the gate."

"An old English custom, I believe. To encourage the others. Any particular head you'd like to see up there?"

"Kurt Viner's would do for a start."

Rojas chuckled harshly. "That's what I like about you. Straight to the point. No beating about the bush."

"It didn't take much working out," Manning said as the jeep moved forward. "It couldn't be anyone else."

"A logical deduction. Such a pleasure to deal with a man of intelligence."

The jeep turned in a half-circle and braked sharply before an arched door. They all got out and Rojas said to the driver, "When Lieutenant Motilina arrives with the old man and the girl, tell him to take them straight to my office. I'll be along later."

He went up the steps through the arched doorway and Manning followed, the two guards just behind him. A broad flight of stone steps lifted into the gloom. On the left was the door of what must obviously be the guard-room and Rojas opened it and went inside.

Two soldiers sat at a table playing cards while a young sergeant lay on one of the narrow cots reading a magazine. One of the players cursed and threw down his cards. The other laughed, his hands reaching out for the stake money in the centre of the table, and then he saw Rojas.

They jumped to their feet, one of them knocking over a chair in his haste and the sergeant came forward, buttoning his tunic hurriedly.

He clicked his heels together and saluted. "Your pleasure, colonel?"

"Get your keys and take us down below," Rojas said. "I want to look at the man in the vaults."

The young sergeant took a bunch of keys from a board and led the way outside. He flicked on an electric light switch, exposing an iron-barred gate previously shrouded in the shadows and opened it.

A broad flight of shallow stone steps dropped down into darkness and the sergeant switched on another light and led the way. Manning was at once conscious of the extreme cold, and shivered. Water trickled down the walls and dripped constantly from the vaulted stone ceiling, making the flags slippery and treacherous.

Rojas was surprisingly sure-footed and when they

reached the bottom, he paused to light another cigar. "The oldest part of the fortress. 1523. How do you like it?"

"Why don't you cut the polite conversation and get to the point?" Manning said.

"I intend to." Rojas moved after the sergeant. "Tell me, what was the excuse you gave Captain Melos for wanting to come to San Juan? To take a few photographs, wasn't it?"

"You know damn well why I came."

Rojas chuckled, the sound re-echoing eerily between the stone walls. "But of course I do. How stupid of me."

The sergeant halted outside an iron-bound door and unlocked it quickly. He took a flashlight from his pocket, handed it to Rojas and stood to one side.

"After you, my friend," Rojas said.

Manning moved cautiously into the darkness. It was bitterly cold and water splashed over his shoes. As Rojas flicked on the flashlight, a large rat scampered across to a corner and disappeared into a hole.

There was a slight groan from the other side of the room and the beam swung across the wall and came to rest upon a man on a narrow bed. His clothing was soiled and torn and he lay in his own filth, so weak that he could barely move his head.

"The man you were looking for, Señor Manning," Rojas said simply. "Juan Garcia."

Manning looked down at Garcia and felt suddenly sick. Only the eyes moved and the skin was shrivelled and white like that of a corpse. There was dried blood on his face and his mouth was terribly swollen.

Juan, can you hear me?" Rojas said in Spanish. "Señor Manning would like to ask you a few questions."

The mouth opened like a gaping wound, red-raw, already festering, and a moan of animal pain emerged.

Rojas turned to Manning and sighed. "I'm sorry, Señor Manning. He would appear to have lost his tongue."

And then he started to laugh, his body shaking, and the sound rebounded between the narrow walls and echoed along the corridor into the darkness. Even the guards look scared and fingered their sub-machine-guns uneasily as Manning stumbled outside. Rojas nodded to the sergeant who locked the cell and they retraced their steps.

When they returned to the guardroom, Lieutenant Motilina was standing by the window drinking coffee and smoking a cigarette. Rojas dropped into a chair on the other side of the table from the door and took off his hat.

"The coffee smells good." Motilina snapped his fingers and one of the soldiers hurriedly poured coffee into another cup and brought it across.

"The old man and the girl, they are upstairs?"

"In the waiting room outside your office."

"I'll deal with them shortly," Rojas said. "First, I would like a few words with Señor Manning."

"Any other orders, colonel?"

Rojas nodded. "The man in the vaults, Juan Garcia. He has served his purpose. Take him outside and shoot him. Leave two men here with me."

There was no trace of emotion on Motilina's face. He clicked his heels smartly, saluted and gave the necessary orders. As the door closed, Rojas pointed to the chair in front of him and Manning sat down.

Rojas produced another of his long black cheroots and lit it carefully.

Manning said, "Before we go any further, let's get one thing straight. The old man and the girl had no idea what I really came here for. I sold them a bill of goods about being a photographer looking for a story for an American magazine and they fell for it."

"They are still guilty of a serious crime against the state." Rojas dropped his match into the lieutenant's cup with a faint hiss. "However, they are not important. You are. There are one or two questions I should like you to answer."

"You're wasting your time."

"I don't think so. I am already extremely well informed about you and your associates. But there are things you could tell me. This C.I.A. man, Morrison, who briefed you for your mission. He must have given you useful contacts. People on the island you could go to in case of need?"

"Try Kurt Viner," Manning said. "He might be able to help you. I can't."

"For technical reasons which should be sufficiently obvious, his message was rather brief. I'm relying on you to fill in the gaps."

Manning shrugged. "As I said before, you're wasting your time."

He was suddenly conscious of the black eyes staring at him unwinkingly. They were cold and hard and full of purpose. Rojas raised a hand and snapped his fingers.

Immediately, the two soldiers at the door, rushed forward and pinioned Manning's arms behind the chair.

"I think it is perhaps time you realized I mean business," Rojas said.

He inhaled deeply on his cigar, leaned forward and touched the glowing end to Manning's right cheek. Manning squirmed, trying to turn his face sideways, but the soldiers leaned their weight against the chair, pushing him hard against the table.

He breathed deeply and tried to hang on. Rojas had stopped smiling. His eyes were fixed and staring, his face wet with sweat and the great fleshy mouth trembled slightly.

And then the agony was too much to bear and Manning cried out and pushed with all his strength against the table. One of the soldiers slipped to one knee, losing his grip, and the chair went over backwards. Manning got to his feet, swung a wild punch at the man on the floor and lunged for the door. As he touched the handle, the other soldier moved in fast and swung the butt of his machine-gun into the small of his back.

Manning crouched on the floor against the wall, waves of pain flooding through his body, and struggled for breath. Faintly through the roaring he was aware that Rojas was laughing.

"Stubborn people, the English," he said in Spanish, "but he will learn. Bring him upstairs."

Manning had grazed his head against the wall in falling and blood trickled into his eye. He brushed it away with one hand and the soldiers jerked him roughly to his feet and followed Rojas through the door.

They mounted the stone steps and turned along a flagged corridor. Outside a door at the far end, a sentry was standing and he opened it quickly.

Anna and her father were sitting on a wooden bench against the wall. Rojas walked past them, opened another door, went in and closed it behind him. One of the soldiers gave Manning a push forward and they stationed themselves by the door.

Manning's brain was still not functioning properly. He staggered against the wall, almost losing his balance and leaned against the whitewashed stonework.

"Are you all right, Harry?" Anna asked anxiously.

"Only just. They're a pretty rough crowd."

The blood from the graze on his forehead trickled down the whitewashed wall, a vivid splash of colour, and he slumped to the bench and managed a tired grin.

Papa Melos looked angry. "They'd better remember we're British citizens, that's all. They can't hold us here indefinitely. We've done nothing wrong."

"That kind of talk went out with the last of the gunboats," Manning said. "The British Government doesn't mean a thing to this bunch."

"We'll see about that."

Anna folded her handkerchief into a pad and dabbed at the blood on Manning's forehead. He smiled. "Worried?"

"Not as much as I should be."

He took one of her hands and said awkwardly. "I'm sorry, Anna. I got you into this mess and right now, I can't see any way out."

"Not your fault, son," Papa Melos cut in. "We knew what we were doing."

Before Manning could reply, the door to the colonel's office opened and a small, seedy-looking clerk in a rumpled gaberdine suit appeared.

He jerked his head. "Inside, all of you." They got to their feet and moved past him, and the guards followed.

The room was panelled in sapele wood and simply furnished with a plain desk and a carpet that covered the floor wall-to-wall. Rojas was standing by the window and he turned, his face serious, and sat behind his desk. He leafed through some papers then looked up at Manning.

"I asked you a question a short time ago. At that time you seemed unwilling to co-operate."

"I still am," Manning said flatly.

Rojas picked up a pen, wrote something on a pad in front of him and put the pen down again.

He turned to Papa Melos. "I have considered your offence most carefully and am prepared to believe you were the unwitting tool of this man. Under the circumstances, I have decided to be lenient. You and your daughter will be released, the boat will be confiscated."

A shudder seemed to pass through the old man's body and his head moved slightly from side-to-side as if he found difficulty in understanding what Rojas had said. Anna moved forward quickly.

"But this is monstrous. We have done nothing! Nothing!"

Rojas arched his eyebrows in surprise. "Is it nothing to bring an American spy into our country? The agent of an unfriendly nation?"

She flinched, the shock of it like a physical blow. Slowly she turned and looked at Manning. "Harry?"

There was nothing he could say and Rojas laughed harshly. "So you believed his story, my dear. How very unfortunate."

She rushed forward, grabbing Manning by the shirt and cried desperately, "It isn't true, Harry. It can't be. The boat's all we've got. All we've got left in the world. Tell him it isn't true!"

"I'm sorry, Anna," He said.

She slapped him across the face with all her strength and then again with the other hand. He didn't defend himself and Rojas barked an order. The two soldiers moved in quickly and pulled her away. One of them pushed her out through the door, the other shoved Papa Melos after her. The old man moved like an automaton, his feet dragging across the floor, and Rojas laughed.

"Surprising how little it takes to break a man."

"For God's sake, give them the boat and let them go," Manning said.

"To salve your conscience?" Rojas shook his head. "A man must be prepared to pay for his mistakes."

"But what will they do? How will they get home?"

"That's their problem." Rojas smiled gently. "The girl's attractive enough. She should be able to think of something." The telephone on his desk rang and he picked it up and nodded to the two soldiers who had returned. "Take him outside. I'll deal with him later."

The little clerk worked at his desk in one corner, his pen scratching monotonously across the paper and Manning sat on the bench against the wall and waited. There was a bad pain in the small of the back and he touched it gently with his fingertips and winced.

He thought of Anna and her father, wondering what would happen to them, but there was nothing he could do. He couldn't even help himself. The two guards stood stolidly on each side of the door and clerk continued to write, and gradually, the shadows lengthened as the sun went down.

One of the soldiers switched on the light, and soon after, the door opened and Rojas came out. He was carrying his hat and cane and when he saw Manning, he smiled.

"I knew there was something. Take Señor Manning to the Special Section. Tell Cienaga to put him in the Hole. I'll deal with him personally tomorrow."

"But there is already a prisoner in the Hole, colonel," the little clerk said.

Rojas frowned. "Who is it?"

The clerk glanced furtively at Manning and then whispered into his chief's ear. Rojas laughed harshly and placed the Panama on his head, pulling the brim down over his eyes.

"Put them together by all means. The situation, while ironic, is full of possibilities." He opened the door and turned. "Till tomorrow, Manning. Think about what I said.

They pulled Manning to his feet and took him out into the corridor and along to the far end. There was a stone staircase built into the wall and at the top, an iron grille. The guard on the other side glanced out and then unlocked it. They walked along a broad passage past several cell doors and came to another iron gate. Again, a guard inspected them before opening it.

They walked along a dark section of passage and emerged onto a long gallery. Chicken wire had been fastened across the pillars from floor to ceiling, but far below, Manning could see the main hall of the fortress.

The roof arched to a centre point supported by great oaken beams, black with age, which lifted from a narrow stone ledge at each end of the great hall. On the other side he could see a similar gallery, but without the chicken wire.

They reached the end of the gallery and paused outside another iron gate. The soldier who unlocked it looked enquiringly at Manning and then opened a door on the left and called, "Cienaga! They've brought you another one."

The man who emerged from the room was short and squat with a great breadth of shoulder and arms so long that the fingertips almost reached the level of his knees. His face was one of the most brutal Manning had ever seen, long, greasy hair hanging to shoulder-length on either side. At some time in the past, his nose had been smashed so badly that it was now almost flat, and tiny black eyes glittered malevolently.

He carried a bunch of keys and hitched at his pants as he came forward. "And what have we here?"

"Englishman," one of the guards said. "Colonel Rojas wants you to put him in the Hole with the other one. Says he'll be up to deal with him tomorrow."

"Englishman, eh?" Cienaga sucked in his breath sharply and spat full in Manning's face. "Pig!"

Something snapped inside Manning at the feel of the cold slime on his cheek. All his pent-up rage and fury erupted in one beautiful punch that swung all the way from the waist and connected with the side of the Cuban's. jaw.

Both soldiers moved a split second later. One gun butt thudded into his back, the other glanced from the side of his head. There was a moment of searing pain and then darkness flooded in on him.

12

Enter Comrade Orlov

He drifted up from a deep pit of darkness into a place of shadows. He was lying on an iron cot from which the mattress had been removed and the springs dug painfully into his back.

It was almost dark outside and a shaft of grey light drifted in through a narrow slot in the stone wall, giving definition to the room, but no more. It was bitterly cold and he pushed himself up and swung his legs to the floor. Immediately, he was conscious of the pain and touched the side of his head gently and found clotted blood.

"Who's there?" he said sharply.

"Ah, English?" the other said, speaking with a slight accent that Manning couldn't place. "How interesting."

"Isn't it just?" Manning said. "And who the hell might you be?"

The man moved across and sat beside him. "Sergei Orlov, Major, 31st Regiment of Engineers."

"A Russian?" Manning said in amazement.

"Georgian," Orlov corrected. "There's a difference, you know."

"So I've heard." Manning held out his hand. "I'm Harry Manning. We may differ in politics, but it certainly looks as if we're in one hell of a spot together. Where are we exactly?"

"They call this cell the Hole," Orlov said. "It's rather unpleasant. Set in the thickness of the fortress walls. If you think it's cold now, wait until the small hours of the morning. No food, no lights, no mattress."

"A sort of preliminary softening-up?"

The Russian nodded. "I'm afraid so. Pity you can't see how elegant it all is. You'll have to wait till dawn for that pleasure."

Manning's hand instinctively went to his breast pocket and found his lighter. "Surprised they didn't take this," he said and flicked it on.

The face that leapt out of the darkness at him was wedge-shaped, the skin drawn tightly over high cheekbones. The eyes were black and flecked with amber and seemed constantly to change colour in the flickering light. The mobile mouth and dark fringe of beard both combined to give an extraordinary impression of vitality.

"They probably forgot to search you in the excitement of beating you up," he said. "I don't suppose you happen to have a cigarette to go with the light?"

Manning tried his other pocket and found his leather case. There were half a dozen cigarettes in it and he took one himself and gave another to the Russian. He moved into the centre of the room, flicked the lighter again and held it above his head.

The cell was perhaps fifteen feet square with rough stone walls and a flagged floor. The long narrow slot in the wall which was the window measured no more than nine inches across. The two iron cots were the only furniture and the wooden door was plated with steel. There was a small grille and he peered through into the dark corridor.

"Seems quiet enough."

"Until someone breaks down and starts screaming."

"And then I suppose our friend Cienaga goes in and beats hell out of them.

Orlov shook his head. "He never enters a cell without an armed guard, and on the night shift he is on his own."

"So the poor devils just scream themselves into the ground?"

"He likes it that way. Often goes along to the cell and watches through the grille."

Manning turned from the door and held the lighter high above his head. It was then he noticed a couple of stout oak beams running from wall-to-wall about ten feet above the ground. At spaced intervals along their length steel hooks jutted out.

"I wonder what that little lot's for?"

"One can imagine," Orlov said. "I must say I prefer to be elsewhere when Colonel Rojas demonstrates."

Manning slipped his lighter into his pocket and sat down again. "What in hell are you doing here, anyway?"

"About three months ago, I was motoring to a staff conference along the coast road in Camaguey Province, when the car skidded over the cliffs into the sea. I managed to get clear and tried to swim for the shore. There was a strong tide running and I was carried out to sea."

"What happened then?"

"A fishing boat picked me up and brought me here. When Rojas got in touch with Havana and informed them I was still alive, they told him to keep quiet about it and to hang on to me."

"But I don't understand?"

"I'm a missile engineer. A scientist in uniform. That's why they sent me to Cuba in the first place."

"I get the idea," Manning said. "If they can't keep the missiles, at least they'll have an expert in constructing the damned things?"

"Exactly," Orlov said. "But I'm afraid Colonel Rojas and I don't see eye-to-eye on the matter."

"You know, somehow I don't think Moscow would be very pleased about this," Manning said.

"The understatement of the age." Orlov sighed and shook his head. "I shall never understand why we had to become involved with these miserable people in the first place. One of Nikita's more inspired blunders."

"I'll second that."

"And you?" Orlov asked. "Why are you here?"

Under the circumstances, there seemed no reason to make a secret of it and Manning told him the whole story.

When he had finished, Orlov shook his head. "Rojas is obviously determined to have his way with both of us and I should imagine his methods leave a lot to be desired."

Manning got to his feet, went to the door and peered out into the dark corridor. He could just see the iron-barred gate that led into the gallery and light splashed under the door of Cienaga's room.

"What's the chicken wire for?"

"A prisoner jumped into the hall a couple of months ago when he was being taken for questioning. Rojas wasn't too pleased. Flogged the soldiers concerned."

"I noticed a similar gallery on the other side of the hall? There was no wire up there."

"Thats the officers' quarters. They kept me in a room there at first. Treated me quite well until I turned awkward."

"And this is supposed to make you see the light?"

"That's the general idea, but I'm afraid he's picked on the wrong man. My parents were killed in the war and I was a partisan fighter at fifteen. Colonel Rojas may well break his teeth on me."

"Ever thought of getting out?"

Orlov laughed softly. "Frequently, but it's impossible. Even if one got out of the cell there are at least four more gates to pass through, each one locked and guarded."

"But what if one could by-pass the gates?"

"I don't understand."

Manning moved back to the bed and sat down. "The main roof out there is held up by huge beams which are supported by a stone ledge at either end and running the full width of the hall."

"So?"

"An active man could cross that ledge to the officers' quarters."

"A desperate man, you mean. The ledge is perhaps nine inches wide and it's eighty feet down to those flags."

"Would you be willing to try?"

"Certainly, but you've forgotten one small point. It would first be necessary to get out of the cell and onto the gallery. How do you suggest we accomplish this?"

"By getting Cienaga in here and relieving him of his keys."

"But I have already told you," Orlov said patiently. "Cienaga never enters the cells without an armed guard and at night he is on his own. Even if we created a disturbance or started a fight to attract him, he would simply stand outside the door enjoying himself."

"What do you think would happen to him if one of his prisoners committed suicide? One of his special prisoners?"

"Rojas would have his hide?"

"Exactly." Manning stood up, flicked on his lighter and held it to the ceiling. "So what would Cienaga do if he looked through that grille and saw one of us hanging from a hook up there?"

"He would come in," the Russian answered automatically and then the implication of his words seemed to hit him and he jumped to his feet excitedly. "By God, you've got it, Manning. As long as there was a chance of cutting the body down in time, he'd have to come in. His fear of what Rojas might do to him would drive every other thought from his head."

"That's what I thought," Manning said. "I'm only worried about one thing. The noise when we jump him. He's certain to put up a fight."

"No one will take any notice. As I said before, there are rows up here every night."

"Okay, then," Manning said. "All we need now is a way of faking the thing."

"That shouldn't be too difficult. As I am smaller than you, I shall take the post of honour while you scream hysterically at the door. Let me have your belt."

Manning gave it to him and then held up his lighter so that the Russian could work in its glow. He fastened his own belt around his waist under the armpits and then buckled Manning's through it, forming a loop which he pushed round to the back.

He grinned gaily. "I hope to God I'm not too heavy."

Manning grinned back. In spite of the short time they had known each other, a well-defined personality had already emerged. It was that of a brave and aggressive, physically tough man, highly intelligent and with a strong vein of humour never far below the surface. A man it was impossible not to like.

"And now your back," he said.

Manning braced himself and Orlov climbed up quickly and then very carefully balanced on his shoulders. Manning held the lighter at arm's length and then the weight was removed from his shoulders and he turned.

Orlov had one arm around the beam and hung there as he reached for the loop of leather with his free hand. He was obviously immensely strong. He slid the loop over a hook, took a deep breath and gently lowered himself. His body swung with a slight eerie creaking and when he dropped his head to one side, the illusion was complete.

"How do I look?"

"Bloody marvellous," Manning said. "Now hold it like that."

He slipped his lighter into his pocket, turned and started to batter against the door with his clenched fist. As the sound echoed along the corridor, he put his face to the grille and cried out in Spanish, "Cienaga, for God's sake, help! He's killing himself."

A moment later, the door at the end of the corridor was flung open and a band of yellow light cut through the darkness. As Cienaga emerged, a flashlight in his hand, Manning redoubled his efforts.

"For God's sake, hurry! He's killing himself."

Cienaga laughed harshly. "Killing himself, eh? That's a new one."

As the brutal face appeared at the grille, Manning drew back slightly. A second later, the beam of the powerful flashlight pierced the darkness and settled upon the figure of the Russian. His body swayed rhythmically from side-to-side, eyes wide and staring and his tongue protruded between his teeth.

Cienaga gave a cry of dismay and the light was withdrawn. A moment later, the key rattled in the door and it was thrown open. He rushed forward into the room and Orlov reached up, grasped the beam firmly and kicked him in the face with both feet held together.

The Cuban lurched back against the wall and the flashlight fell from his hand and rolled across the floor. He started to get to his feet and Manning moved in to finish him off. He lifted his knee into the smashed and bleeding face and then the great arms fastened around him and started to squeeze.

Manning struggled desperately to free himself as the air was driven from his lungs and then Orlov arrived on the scene. He directed the flashlight onto Cienaga's face then carefully struck him under the right ear with all his force. Cienaga's eyes rolled until only the whites were showing and he released his grip. He keeled over onto his face and Orlov kicked him on the side of the head.

The key was still in the lock, the rest of the bunch hanging from it and they locked the door quickly. They stood listening for a moment or two, but nothing stirred. The gallery was dimly lit and the whole block wrapped in quiet as Manning worked his way through the bunch of keys until he found the right one. They moved outside quickly and locked the gate after them.

Only a single light illuminated the hall below and the roof was shrouded in darkness. The chicken wire presented no problem. Pulling on it between them, they forced it away from the wall making a large enough gap for them to squeeze through.

The first beam lifted from the ledge about three feet to the left. Manning took a deep breath and stepped gingerly across. It was surprisingly easy. He waited until Orlov joined him and then turned his face to the wall, spread out his arms and started to inch his way across.

Time seemed to have no meaning as he moved steadily to the left and it was with a sense of surprise that his fingers touched the next beam. He rested a moment, waiting for Orlov. When the Russian joined him, there was sweat on his face, but he managed a grin.

"Keep moving. We haven't got all night."

There were three more beams to by-pass and Manning moved on, his breathing unnaturally loud in his ears and then a door clanged. He froze to the wall and glanced down in time to see a soldier pass through the pool of light in the hall below. He paused to light a cigarette and then disappeared through a door. Manning started to inch sideways again. A couple of minutes later, he scrambled over the balustrade and stood on the other gallery.

Orlov joined him and they paused in the shadows listening. Somewhere there was laughter as a door opened, silence as it closed again.

"I know my way about on this side of the fortress," Orlov said. "They've installed a service lift at the end of this corridor which goes down to the ground floor where the orderlies have their quarters. We'll stand a better chance of getting out that way. It's at the rear."

Manning nodded and the Russian led the way along the corridor. The lift doors were new and shining and looked strangely out of place. As he pressed the button, Manning noticed with amusement that the manufacturer's plate said *Made in Detroit*, which proved something, though he couldn't think what.

When the lift arrived, they stepped inside quickly and started down. He was conscious of a strange, hollow feeling in his stomach as they came to a halt, but the doors opened into a large, quiet basement. There was no one about.

They moved to the door and turned into a long bightly lit corridor. Voices came from a room to their left and the door was slightly ajar. Manning caught a glimpse of soldiers sitting round a table eating and moved on quickly after Orlov.

The Russian stood listening at one of the doors further on and opened it as Manning arrived. It looked like the quarters of half a dozen men. The beds were ranged around the room, blankets neatly folded. Sub-machine-guns and automatic rifles stood in a rack in one corner and there was a selection of uniforms and other items of equipment in the tin lockers by each bed.

"How good is your Spanish?" Orlov asked.

"Pretty fluent."

Then this is the obvious way out for us."

They dressed quickly in military greatcoats and peaked caps and took a sub-machine-gun each. They went back into the corridor and moved on quickly, mounted several stone steps and came into a narrow corridor that opened into a small hall.

There was a tiny glass office in the entrance and a guard casually leafed through a magazine, a cigarette in his mouth. Manning and Orlov walked out casually, sub-machine-guns slung from their shoulders. As they passed the office, Manning half-raised a hand and the guard waved carelessly in reply.

It was raining outside and they went down some stone steps into a wide courtyard and walked into the darkness. "All the trucks come in here," Orlov said. "We still have to walk round to the front gate. It's the only way out."

Manning touched his arm and pointed. A few yards away, a jeep stood outside a lighted doorway. "The Officers' Mess," the Russian whispered.

"Couldn't be better," Manning said. "Less chance of being questioned."

They moved across the wet cobbles quickly. He climbed behind the wheel and pressed the starter. As the Russian scrambled into the other seat, they moved away.

He waited for the sound to come from behind him, for the sudden cries of alarm, but all was quiet. He turned into the front yard and approached the gate. It was ridiculously easy. When they were still twenty yards away, the guard raised the swing bar. A few moments later, they were driving rapidly through the night, down into San Juan.

13

From the Jaws of the Tyrant

As they turned onto the waterfront, a thin fog rolled in from the harbour, pushed by the wind. Although there were lights in many windows, the streets were deserted and when Manning braked to a halt a few yards from Bayo's place, he was conscious of the extreme quiet.

"Are you sure your friends will be here?" Orlov asked.

"They'd better be. I don't know where else to start looking," Manning said. "You stay here. I'll see how things are."

He approached the hotel and peered in through the window. Bayo stood behind the bar reading a newspaper and three old men played cards in the corner. Otherwise, the place was deserted.

He moved back to Orlov who waited beside the jeep. "No sign of them. Let's hope they're here somewhere."

They moved along a narrow alley at the side of the

building and turned into a cobbled yard. The back door wasn't locked and they stepped into a large, whitewashed kitchen. A small black and white puppy who had been sleeping in a basket in the corner rushed forward and started yapping furiously. As Manning bent down to pat him, the door to the bar opened and Bayo came in.

"Here, what do you want?" he demanded angrily and then he recognized Manning.

He closed the door behind him and leaned against it, crossing himself hurriedly. "Holy Mother aid me."

"You've got nothing to worry about," Manning said in English. "I only want to know what's happened to Papa Melos and Anna."

Bayo was quite obviously terrified. "If Rojas finds I've helped you, he'll take a week over killing me."

"If you're smart, he won't need to know."

The Cuban made an obvious effort to pull himself together, crossed the room and opened another door. "In here."

Papa Melos lay on a bed against the wall, eyes closed, mouth slightly open. There was an empty bottle of rum on the bed, and another had spilled half its contents across the floor so that the whole place stank of liquor.

Orlov bent down, rolled back one of the old man's eyelids and felt his pulse. He turned and shook his head. "He'll be like this for hours."

Manning kicked the empty rum bottle across the floor and turned to Bayo. "How long's he been like this?"

"Several hours. He tried to see Colonel Rojas again about his boat, but they wouldn't let him through the gates. Then he found they'd moved it out into the harbour and put a guard on board. That was when he came back and started on the rum."

"What about the girl?"

"She did her best to stop him, but he wouldn't listen."

"Where is she now?"

"She went to see Colonel Rojas to beg him to return the boat to her father."

"He wouldn't cut his own mother down if she were hanging," Manning said.

"Who knows, señor?" Bayo shrugged. "She is pretty and the colonel's weakness for young girls is well known."

Manning's throat turned dry. He moistened his lips and said, "Where does he live? At the fortress?"

Bayo shook his head. "He has a *hacienda* about a quarter of a mile out of town. Very fine, señor. Set in a walled garden."

"What about guards?"

"There is one on the gate, three inside. And the colonel's aide, Lieutenant Motilina, he lives at the house also. He is personally responsible for his security."

Manning stood there thinking about it and Orlov said, "You are thinking of paying this place a visit?"

Manning nodded. "I'll take the jeep. If I'm not back in an hour I suggest you steal a boat from the harbour and get to hell out of here."

"When we go, we go together," Orlov said. "Besides, I should enjoy meeting Rojas again."

"Then we'd better take the old man with us," Manning said. "From now on, we're going to have to move fast. I wouldn't like to have to leave him behind." He turned to Bayo. "We have a jeep outside."

"I will carry him for you, señor."

Bayo hoisted the old man across his shoulders and they went out through the yard and along the alley to the front of the building. They eased him onto the floor at the rear and Manning and Orlov got in quickly.

Manning switched on the engine and held out his hand. "My thanks, Bayo."

"We have a proverb, señor. Have patience and you will see your enemy's funeral procession. Go with God."

The Cuban turned and disappeared into the alley and Manning drove away quickly.

The wrought iron gates of the *hacienda* stood open and the lamp suspended from the archway above swayed in the wind, a pool of light constantly reaching out into the darkness and retreating again.

The sentry stepped out of his wooden box, raising a hand to halt them. Manning slowed, but kept on moving.

"Urgent dispatch for Colonel Rojas," he called and the sentry waved and stepped back into his box.

The gardens were a riot of colour and palm trees lifted their heads above the wall and gently nodded in the cool breeze, leaves etched against the night sky. The drive curved suddenly and Manning braked to a halt at the front door.

They went up the steps quickly and entered a wide hall, cool and pleasant and very quiet. They could hear voices from a door to the left and someone was singing a popular *guaracha*.

> *Fidel has arrived,*
> *Fidel has arrived,*
> *Now we Cubans are freed*
> *From the jaws of the tyrant.*

When Orlov opened the door, two men were sitting at a table in the centre of the room, tunics unbuttoned, playing chess. A third sat on the edge of a bunk and strummed a guitar.

"On your feet!" Manning said in Spanish.

They stood up slowly, hands clasped behind their necks. Two of them were only boys, but the guitar player was older, with a cold, hard face.

"Where's Motilina?" Manning demanded.

No one replied and he moved forward quickly and rammed the barrel of his sub-machine-gun into the stomach of the boy on the end.

"Where is he?"

"Don't tell him anything," the guitar player said. "They won't get far."

Orlov transferred his machine-gun to his left hand, took a step forward and punched the man in the face. He staggered back, blood spurting from his nose.

The boy said hurriedly, "In the kitchen. It's at the other end of the corridor past the stairs."

"Any servants?"

The boy shook his head. "They have the night off."

"A young girl called earlier. What happened to her?"

105

"She's with the colonel. He said he wasn't to be disturbed."

"Did you get all that?" Manning asked Orlov.

The Russian nodded. "Most of it. You get after the girl. I'll see to these three."

Manning moved quickly along the hall past the stairs that curved up to the second floor and entered a narrow corridor. Light showed under a door at the far end. He stood outside, listening for a moment, and then gently turned the handle. Motilina was frying eggs at the stove, his back to the door. As he turned, reaching for a loaf of bread, he saw Manning and a frown appeared on his face.

"Who are you? What do you want?"

In the same moment, Manning moved forward, reversed his gun and drove the butt into the side of the Cuban's neck. He gave a terrible groan and collapsed against the table, sliding down to the floor where he lay quite still.

Manning wiped sweat from his face and moved outside. Somewhere close at hand, he could hear the murmur of voices. He moved along the corridor, turned a corner and paused at another door. For a moment, there was silence and then someone cried out in pain and Rojas laughed. Manning opened the door and went inside.

The room was pleasantly furnished, the floor covered by a heavy Indian carpet, and the french windows stood open to the night, their curtains lifting in the slight breeze.

Anna was lying across a divan by the stone fireplace and Rojas sprawled across her, his hands moving over the young body. She moaned and Rojas chuckled again. Manning moved silently across the thick carpet and tapped him on the shoulder. As Rojas turned in surprise, he jerked him away from her and drove his fist into the fleshy mouth with all his force.

Rojas staggered back against the divan and Anna scrambled to her feet and moved to Manning. Her dress was torn at the neck and there was a smear of blood on her mouth, but otherwise, she seemed all right.

"No questions," Manning said. "Outside."

She ran for the door and he backed across the room

slowly, menacing Rojas with the sub-machine-gun. The Cuban stayed where he was, a hand to his smashed mouth, and Manning backed into the corridor where Anna was leaning against the wall waiting for him.

"All right?"

She nodded. "I knew what I was doing."

"Straight out of the front door," he said. "You'll find your father in the rear of the jeep that's parked at the bottom of the steps."

She turned at once and hurried along the corridor and Manning stepped back into the room. Rojas was on his feet and reaching for the telephone that stood on a small coffee table near the divan.

"I don't think so," Manning said.

Rojas straightened slowly, his face quite calm. "You won't even get off the island, Manning."

Manning fired from the hip and the bullets smacked into the Cuban's body. As he spun round, a long burst drove him across the divan and his jacket burst into flames.

As Manning ran along the corridor, he heard shooting and Orlov backed out of the guard room firing from the hip. They went down the steps on the run and scrambled into the jeep. Anna was already in the rear, crouched beside her father, and Manning switched on the engine and drove away rapidly.

As he rounded the curve of the drive, the sentry was running towards them. Manning accelerated, swinging the wheel so that they swerved, and the man jumped into the bushes.

As they turned out through the gate, he said to Orlov, "What happened back there?"

The Russian shrugged. "The guitar-player took a chance and tried to grab a rifle from the rack. What about Rojas?"

"Met with a nasty accident."

Anna moved behind him and put a hand on his shoulder. "I don't understand all this, Harry. What's been happening?"

"No time to explain now," he said, "we'll leave that till we're safe on board the *Cretan Lover* and well out to sea."

"We're getting the boat back?"

107

"We're going to have a bloody good try. This is Sergei Orlov, by the way. We got out of the fortress together."

A smile of great charm appeared on the Russian's face and he held out his hand. "How's your father?"

Before she could reply, they roared along the waterfront and Manning changed down and turned on to the jetty. He braked to a halt at the end and jumped out.

The fog was thicker now, rolling up from the water in long opaque fingers. The *Cretan Lover* was anchored about fifty yards out into the harbour and he unbuttoned his greatcoat quickly.

"You intend to swim?" Orlov said.

Manning nodded. "Take too long to look for a dinghy and there's a guard on board. I don't want to advertise."

He lowered himself into the cold water and started to swim in a powerful but quiet breast-stroke out into the harbour. When he was only a few feet away from the *Cretan Lover*, a strange unearthly wailing sounded from the battlements of the fortress, echoing away into the night in a dying fall. It was obviously a siren sounding the general alarm and a soldier emerged from the cabin of the *Cretan Lover* and rushed to the rail.

Manning took a deep breath and swam down under the boat, the keel scraping his back. He surfaced on the other side beside the short diving ladder and hauled himself up quickly. He moved across the deck silently and pushed the guard over the rail into the water, then ran to the stern and hauled the anchor in by hand.

On shore, all hell seemed to have broken loose and he could see the lights of several vehicles moving down the road from the fortress. The anchor came over the side unexpectedly and he dropped it to the deck and ran into the wheelhouse.

At first, when he pressed the starter, nothing happened. He tried again, holding the button down desperately, and suddenly the engine coughed and spluttered into life.

As he ran alongside the jetty, two jeeps turned onto the waterfront. The rail scraped protestingly against the piles and Anna jumped down and turned to catch her father as Orlov lowered him. As the Russian followed,

108

Manning took the boat away in a burst of speed.

As he moved into the channel, Orlov joined him in the wheelhouse. "Do you think they'll come after us?"

Manning shook his head. "There wasn't anything in harbour fast enough. It's the pill-box they've got on the point at the mouth of the channel that I'm worried about. If the thing's manned, we may be in for trouble."

"I'll get the old man and the girl down into the cabin," Orlov said, "then I'll come back. Perhaps a little answering fire will cool their ardour."

Manning strained his eyes into the mist. They passed the fortress on the left and he could see the dark headland jutting out into the sea and suddenly a great coloured stream of tracer soared into the night from their right.

"Heavy machine-gun," Orlov cried as he rushed in. "Keep moving. I'll handle them."

The boat shuddered as a stream of bullets thudded into her hull and Orlov leaned out of the side window and returned the fire with his sub-machine-gun. For a little, the Cubans answered and then, quite suddenly, they stopped.

A few moments later, the *Cretan Lover* ran out into the open sea.

14

Exuma Sound

The water was being whipped into whitecaps by a strong east wind that blew steadily out to sea carrying the fog before it. Visibility was becoming better minute-by-minute and after a while, the moon moved from behind a cloud.

Manning took a quick look at the chart and altered course several points as Orlov came in.

"What's the situation below?"

"The old man's still unconscious. The girl's seeing to him now."

"Any damage?"

"Bullet holes all over the place. Good thing she had the sense to get down on the floor."

"She's quite a girl," Manning said.

The Russian nodded and glanced down at the chart. "Where are we making for?"

"Spanish Cay. I think Morrison would like to know

about Kurt Viner as soon as possible."

"Have we enough fuel?"

"We filled the tanks before leaving Harmon Springs. That gives us a range of more than seven hundred miles."

"Good enough," Orlov said. "I'd appreciate a bath and about fifteen hours in a decent bed."

Manning glanced sideways at him. "You're not worried at all?"

"Why should I be? All the authorities in Nassau can do is pass me on to our ambassador when they hear my story."

"Perhaps they won't want to let you go."

The Russian grinned. "Don't think the thought hasn't occurred to me. After all, men with my background *are* at a premium. I could probably teach the gentlemen at Canaveral a useful trick or two."

"They wouldn't like that sort of talk in the Kremlin at all."

Orlov smiled again. "But I'm not in Moscow, am I? Would you like me to take the wheel for a while?"

"Think you can handle her?"

"I've had experience."

"All right. Try and get some sleep. Come back up in about three hours. We'll spell each other through the night."

When the Russian had gone, he pulled the seat from the wall, suddenly drained of all his strength. The wheelhouse seemed unbearably warm and he opened a window and leaned out, breathing deeply on the good salt air.

The door creaked open and closed again. Without turning, he was acutely aware of her presence.

"Coffee, Harry?"

He held the mug in one hand and drank the contents down, grateful for the new life it gave him. "How's your father?"

"He'll be all right. It's happened before."

"Once too often can kill a man."

"All sorts of things can do that," she said calmly. "Cigarette? I found a packet in the cabin."

He took one gratefully. A match flared in her cupped

111

hands illuminating her face as he leaned forward for a light. She had never looked more lovely and he instinctively put out a hand and touched her cheek.

And then she was tight in his arms, her face turned up to him. "Why, Harry? Why?"

He held her close, one hand on the wheel, and explained about Maria Salas and how she had died and of the trail he had followed to Nassau that had ended with the death of Pelota.

When he had finished, she was silent for a while. "You must have loved her a great deal?"

"I'm not even sure what the word means any more," he said. "I only know I was going downhill fast and she pulled me back. I owe her something for that at least."

There was another small silence and she said. "What happens now?"

"We make for Spanish Cay. I must tell Morrison about Viner as soon as possible."

"And afterwards, when the whole thing's over and done with?"

"Who knows? I'll think of something."

For a little while longer, she stayed within the circle of his arms and then she pulled herself free and crossed to the door. "I'll see how Papa is."

"It's no good, Anna," Manning said quietly. "I'm twenty years too old for you."

"I wouldn't be too sure about that," she said and the door closed softly behind her.

She had left the packet of cigarettes on the chart table and he lit one and sighed heavily. Life was like the circles rain made on the surface of a pond, constantly running into each other. No sooner had a man moved out of one situation than he found himself up to his neck in another. He settled back in his chair, moved course a point to the east and concentrated on his steering.

Orlov relieved him at one a.m. and he went below. Papa Melos was still out cold and Anna was sleeping peacefully, her head pillowed on one arm. He flopped down on the spare bunk and stared up at the bulkhead, thinking about everything, but great waves of tiredness

112

swept over him. Within a few minutes, he was sleeping soundly.

He came awake to an insistent pressure on his shoulder and looked up into Anna's anxious face. He sat up quickly and swung his legs to the floor.

"What is it?"

"Something's wrong with the boat. She's not handling right. Sergi wants you on deck."

It was then he noticed her father sitting huddled at the table, a mug of coffee in his hands. "How do you feel?"

The old man's face was grey and wrinkled, the eyes like black holes, but he managed a ghastly grin. "Better get up top and see what's wrong."

The boat was rolling sluggishly, that much was self-evident as Manning went up the companionway, and her speed was greatly reduced. As he went out on deck, a strong east wind dashed spray in his face, but the sky was still clear and visibility good as the moon travelled towards the horizon.

The Russian turned from the wheel, an expression of relief on his face. "I don't know what's wrong, but something is."

Manning took over. The steering was sluggish and heavy and yet the throttle was fully open. He turned to Orlov, "Keep her as steady as you can and I'll check the engine."

As he went back on deck, Anna emerged from the companionway. "Better have a look below, Harry."

Manning followed her down to the cabin and paused in the doorway. A good inch of water slopped across the floor and Papa Melos had the hatch open.

He turned and shook his head. "She's filling up fast, Harry. There must be a hole in her somewhere."

"Probably that blasted machine gun when we were running out of San Juan," Manning said. "Where's the pump?"

"In the stern," Anna told him. "I'll show you. I'm afraid it's only hand-operated."

He groaned. "That's all we needed."

113

He crouched in the stern while Anna held a flashlight and primed the pump and then got to work, swinging the lever vigorously until a stream of discoloured water gushed across the deck and over the side.

He changed hands frequently and, after half an hour, there was a noticeable change in the way the boat was behaving. He handed over to Anna and went into the wheelhouse.

"Keep her moving at full speed," he told Orlov. "It looks as if we sustained some damage below the waterline running out of San Juan. I'm going to take a look."

When he went below, Papa Melos had the hatch cover off again and was peering into the scuppers. He turned and nodded.

"Still plenty there, but nothing like as bad."

"I'll go in and take a look," Manning said.

He had perhaps three feet in which to move and there was a good eighteen inches of water slopping over the ribs. He went in feet first, the flashlight between his teeth, acutely aware of the stench that is always to be found in any ship's bilge. He moved forward on his hands and knees holding the flashlight above his head.

As the boat lifted over the waves, the level of the water rose and fell, slapping across his face, on one occasion passing right over his head, soaking him to the skin.

There were several ragged bullet holes in the bows and water oozed in constantly. He examined them for a moment and then moved back and pulled himself through the hatch into the cabin.

"How bad is it?" the old man said.

"Could be worse. After all, it's almost seven hours since we left San Juan so it took its time to get as bad as it did. Another three hours and we'll be in Spanish Cay. We'll get her fixed up there. You've nothing to worry about."

The old man was still pretty groggy. He sat down and reached for the coffee pot and Manning went back up on deck. The wind had freshened considerably and clouds scudded across the face of the moon. As he went into the wheelhouse, rain spattered against the glass.

"How bad is it?" Orlov said.

"It's coming in pretty slowly at the moment. That's why it took so long to show."

"How long till we reach Spanish Cay?"

"Three hours."

"Then we've no worries."

"I wouldn't be too sure. The side of the cabin's like a sieve, remember. If we run into dirty weather, we won't stay afloat for long."

Orlov looked anxiously out through the window at the rain. "What do you think?"

"Let's say it doesn't look too promising," Manning told him. "I'd better take over here. You give Anna a spell on that pump and keep it working."

During the next half hour the weather deteriorated rapidly and visibility was considerably reduced. The *Cretan Lover* lurched over the waves, spray scattering the length of her deck, and after a while, she started to ship water.

The door opened and Papa Melos came in and slammed it shut. In the light from the binnacle, he looked much more his old self.

"How's she handling?"

"Not too well," Manning said. "I think she's filling up again."

"I'll take over. You go and check."

Manning went outside and moved along the deck. In the weird glow of the green and red navigation lights, he could see Orlov crouched by the pump in the cabin, working rhythmically.

When he went down into the cabin, he found Anna on one of the bunks, desperately trying to plug the bullet holes with pieces of rag. Each time a wave dashed against the hull, great fingers of water syphoned into the cabin. There was already at least six inches on the floor.

"Do what you can," he said. "I'll be back in a little while."

He went and crouched beside Orlov, the wind carrying away his voice so that he had to shout into the Russian's ear.

"Can you keep it up?"

"I think so. How are we doing?"

"Not so good. I'm going to check on our position."

As he moved along the deck, a great sea passed over the rail, knocking him onto his back, and he slid against the engine-room hatch and bruised his shoulder. He scrambled to his feet and staggered towards the wheel-house, using the rail to force his way along.

When he went in, the old man turned, his face grim. "It's taking her all her time to breast these waves."

"There's water pouring in all over the place down below," Manning told him. "Anna's doing what she can to stop it. See if you can help her. I'll take over here for a while."

The old man nodded, relinquishing the wheel. When he had gone, Manning slumped into the seat and leaned his forehead on the window pane. He was tired and scared and very cold. Beyond the navigation lights there was nothing, only the darkness and the wind which moaned around the wheelhouse, filling him with foreboding.

He was tired. Too tired to think straight and yet he had to. He flicked on the light above the chart table and holding the wheel with one hand, tried to work out their position.

By now they were well into Exuma Sound and north was Eleuthera, but how far north? He didn't have much to go on and worked out a dead reckoning based on their speed and approximate mileage. The result seemed to indicate that he should alter course to north-west for Spanish Cay, but north of Exuma there were hundreds of rocks and cays. In weather like this, they wouldn't stand a chance.

He compromised and altered course half a point. Gradually, a faint pearly luminosity appeared and he was able to distinguish the dark, silver lances of the rain. Half an hour later, dawn came and he opened the window and looked out at leaden clouds hurrying across the sky.

The wind was fading and already the waves were calmer, but the *Cretan Lover* was moving at no more than a couple of knots. Each time she dipped into a trough, Manning thought she would never lift again.

The door opened and Papa Melos entered. He was soaked to the skin and looked on the point of collapse. "No good, Harry. We aren't getting anywhere."

"If my calculations are correct, we can't be far from one of the cays north of Exuma," Manning said. "Take over and keep her on the same course."

Orlov still crouched by the pump, arms moving monotonously, but he looked as if he couldn't last out much longer. Manning started down the companionway and stepped into water that immediately rose to the level of his thighs.

Anna was in the act of sliding from a bunk and she lurched towards him. "It's no good, Harry. She's going to go down."

Her face was drawn and she was bitterly cold. He took a reefer jacket from behind the door, slipped it over her shoulders and they went up the companionway together.

"Go into the wheelhouse, you'll be warmer in there," he said. "I'm going to help Orlov."

The wind had dropped almost completely and the sky was clearing fast, but a strong swell was still running. He crouched beside the Russian and took over the pump, keeping up the rhythm.

Orlov flexed his cramped hands and shook his head. "You're wasting your time. It's coming in at three times the rate. She won't last much longer."

At the same moment, the engines stopped. There was a sudden hiss as if gas were escaping and a great cloud of steam rose through the vents in the engine-room hatch.

The *Cretan Lover* wallowed sluggishly, hardly lifting as the swell undulated across the surface of the sea and Papa Melos and Anna came out of the wheelhouse. The old man looked tired and defeated and she was holding his arm as if to support him.

"I'm sorry," Manning said. "More sorry than you'll ever know."

"You did your best, boy. You're a fine sailor."

They unshipped the dinghy and slid it over the side. Anna and her father sat in the stern, Manning and Orlov took an oar each.

By now, the sea was at deck-level and as they started to row away, it slopped across the planks in a green curtain. After a while, they rested on their oars and sat there waiting.

The stern of the old boat dipped beneath the waves, the bows lifting out of the water. For a moment, it poised there at an angle and then slid smoothly under.

There was nothing left to say and Manning started to row, fixing his gaze on a point somewhere beyond the old man and the girl, trying to avoid looking at either of them.

Gradually, the sky turned blue and the sun came out and low on the horizon to the north-west, they could see land. Two hours later they were picked up by old man Saunders out of Spanish Cay after tuna with a Negro deckhand.

15

At the Caravel

As he walked along the jetty towards the *Grace Abounding* Manning could see Seth standing in the stern coiling a rope. He hung it on a hook outside the wheelhouse, waved to a passing launch and went below.

Manning was hot and tired. Too hot to wait for the others. He glanced over his shoulder to make sure they were coming and jumped down to the deck. For a moment, he paused, looking about him with a conscious pleasure before going down into the coolness of the air-conditioned cabin. Seth was in the galley and Manning could smell coffee.

"Better get another four cups out," he said. "You've got company."

He slumped down on the padded bench seat and Seth moved out of the galley and frowned at him. "Man, you look like hell."

"I'm not surprised," Manning said. "That's exactly where I've been. These days they call it Cuba."

Seth's eyes widened. "So you made it into San Juan? Did you find Garcia?"

"What was left of him. As it turned out, they were waiting for me to arrive."

Seth looked bewildered. "But that ain't possible, Harry. Only the three of us knew you were going. I know I ain't no Cuban spy and Morrison can't be. That only leaves Mr. Viner."

"Exactly!"

Before the Negro could reply, a step sounded on the companionway and Orlov entered, followed by Anna and her father.

"Some friends I picked up along the way," Manning said. "I think they'd appreciate a little of that coffee."

Seth hurried into the galley and Anna and her father subsided onto the other bench seat. They both looked completely exhausted.

Manning gave Orlov a cigarette and pushed the packet across the table to Anna. "How do you feel?"

There were dark smudges under her eyes and her face was very white, but she managed a smile. "Nothing a few hours' sleep won't cure."

"There's a shower and two cabins aft. Seth will show you where. Maria left a few dresses and things in one of them. You're welcome to help yourself."

Her father had sunk into a state of complete apathy and huddled in the corner, head bowed. She spoke to him in a low voice and then turned anxiously to Manning. "I think he should lie down. Could we take him along to the cabin now?"

Manning started to rise, but Orlov beat him to it. "I'll give you a hand," he said, helping the old man to his feet, and they took him out through the galley.

Manning sat there, his head in his hands, great waves of tiredness sweeping through him. When the coffee came, it was so hot that it scalded his mouth, but for the moment, it gave him new life and the ability to think straight for a little longer.

When Orlov and Anna returned, Seth brought them fresh coffee and Manning said, "Seen Morrison lately?"

Seth nodded. "We were out Cat Island way yesterday. He asked me to run him over to Nassau this afternoon. He's still at the Caravel. Same room."

"Is Joe Howard in town?"

Seth shook his head. "He left for Crab Cay early this morning with both his constables. They found some guy with a knife in his back over there last night."

Manning finished his coffee and stood up. "I think I'll go and see Morrison."

He opened the map drawer in the table, rummaged beneath some charts and took out a Luger automatic and a Smith & Wesson .38 revolver with a sawn-off barrel. He hefted them both in his hands for a moment, decided on the Luger and replaced the Smith & Wesson in the drawer.

"You are expecting trouble?" Orlov said.

Manning pushed the Luger down into his waistband beneath his shirt. "You never can tell."

"Then I think I shall come with you."

Anna had been sitting watching them, her coffee still untasted. She stood up. "What about us, Harry?"

"You stay here. I've still got a room at the Caravel. That'll do Orlov and me for the time being. After I've seen Morrison I'll be back for my things. You can leave as soon as you like after that. If you think you could do with him, Seth can crew for you as far as Harmon Springs."

There was a slight frown on her face. "I don't understand."

"I'm giving you the boat," he said. "The way I see it, it's the least I owe you." She swayed, clutching at the edge of the table, and he gave Orlov a little push towards the companionway. "Let's get moving."

The Russian went first and Manning followed. As they climbed to the jetty, Anna stumbled out on deck.

"No, Harry! No!"

He said calmly, "No arguments, Anna. That's the way it's going to be."

She started to cry helplessly, leaning against the wheelhouse, her face to the wall and he turned and found Orlov looking at him gravely. "I think you are a very great fool, my friend."

"That's the way it goes," Manning said. "Sometimes you win—sometimes you lose."

Everything that was in him, every fibre of his being urged him to go back, to tell her that this was what he truly wanted, but he was involved enough already. He had done Anna Melos and her father a great wrong. Now he had made up for it. Let it end there.

The terrace of the Caravel was crowded with tourists dining in the open under the shade of the sea-almond trees and a Negro steel band played and sang a calypso on the lawn below.

As Manning moved across to the reception desk, the Negro clerk saw him coming and grinned. "Good to see you, Mr. Manning."

Manning helped himself to a cigarette from the box on the desk. "Mr. Viner said he'd hold Señorita Salas's old room for me."

"That's right, sir." The clerk took a key down from the board. "You going up now?"

Manning nodded. "Is Mr. Viner around?"

"I believe he's in his office. I'd be glad to phone through and check for you."

Manning shook his head. "I'll see him later. Right now I need a shower more than anything else."

He went upstairs quickly, Orlov at his heels, and moved along the carpeted corridor to Maria's room. The shades were drawn and the bed had been freshly made. It was cool and dark and he stood there listening for something, aware of a feeling of unreality so strong that it took a conscious effort to pull himself out of it.

"Bath and a shower through there," he told Orlov. "Clean clothes in the wardrobe. Just help yourself."

"You're going to see Morrison?"

"No sense in wasting time."

Morrison's room was on the next floor. He went upstairs quickly and paused outside the door. He knocked softly, opened it and went in.

122

"Put it on the table, son. I'll be right in," Morrison called from the terrace.

Manning waited, a slight smile on his face. When the American appeared he was wearing only a towel wrapped around his waist. He carried a book in one hand, sunglasses in the other. When he saw Manning, a look of complete astonishment appeared on his face.

"Well I'll be damned. I thought it was room service."

There was another knock on the door and Manning moved quickly into the bathroom. He heard the door open, the murmur of voices, and it closed again. When he emerged, Morrison was putting a tray containing a half bottle of whiskey and a jug of ice-water on the table.

"There should be a tooth glass in there somewhere."

Manning found the glass, rinsed it and went back into the bedroom. Morrison was standing at the window looking out to sea. He turned and nodded towards the tray.

"Help yourself."

Manning half-filled his glass with whiskey, topped it with ice-water and took it down in two easy swallows. He shook his head, slumped into a chair and reached for the bottle again.

"You look as if you've been through the mill," Morrison said. "Did you manage to get a boat in Harmon Springs?"

"I got a boat all right. I even got into San Juan." Manning swallowed some more of his whisky. "A waste of time. The man I should really have been looking for was back here on Spanish Cay."

Morrison frowned. "What are you trying to say?"

"That Kurt Viner's in this business right up to his neck."

Morrison moved across to the wardrobe, took out a suit and a fresh shirt and threw them on the bed. "Tell me about it while I dress. Everything, mind you. Don't leave a damned thing out. This could be more important than you know."

Manning helped himself to another drink and started to talk. It didn't take long and when he had finished, Morrison was standing in front of the mirror fastening his tie.

He reached for his coat. "And this guy Orlov, you've got him downstairs now?"

Manning nodded. "Never mind him. What about Viner? What do you think?"

Morrison shook his head. "Hard to say. For what it's worth, I don't see him as anything more than a front man. The rest of them, the really important ones, are out there somewhere, just waiting."

"But waiting for what?" Manning said. "And how can you be sure they're still around?"

"They sabotaged another tracker station the day you left. Better than a million dollars' worth of damage and not a trace of them."

"Then the solution's obvious. Call out the Marines, the Navy, anything it takes. You're bound to find them in the end."

Morrison shook his head. "You said it yourself. Seven hundred islands, two thousand cays and rocks. It could take weeks and we can't stand a stink at this time. The top brass aren't due till next week, but our Secretary of State and your own Foreign Secretary start their preliminary talks at the Lyford Cay Club tomorrow. That's about fifteen miles from Nassau. For the next few days, these islands are going to be the focus of world attention."

"And you think our friends might try to pull another stunt at the worst possible moment."

"Something like that."

Manning was beginning to feel slightly tight. He carefully poured another measure of whisky into his glass, drank it down and grinned. "There's only one sure way of finding out."

"And what's that?"

"I'll ask Viner."

"You sure you know what you're doing?"

Manning nodded. "I'll introduce you to Orlov on the way, but don't try to pump him. The only time he'll ever open his mouth is if he feels like it."

There was no sign of Orlov when they went downstairs, but they could hear him splashing about in the bathroom. When Manning opened the door, clouds of steam billowed out. Orlov was immersed to the chin in hot water, a blissful expression on his face.

"You look happy," Manning said.

Orlov grinned. "It doesn't take much. Do they have chambermaids here?"

"Not in the afternoons. Wrong climate. You'll have to make do with Morrison. Maybe you'll find more in common than either of you realize."

He left them there and went downstairs. He was feeling strangely light-headed and realized with something of a shock that he hadn't eaten for more than thirty-six hours. No wonder the whisky had gone straight to his head.

People who had dined well were filled with a false sense of security so the casino was always busy in the early afternoon. Manning pushed his way through the crowd towards the green baize door and was aware of the little manager moving to cut him off.

He just made it and grinned falsely. "Looking for someone, Mr. Manning?"

"You know damn well I am."

"I'm afraid Mr. Viner's busy right now. He's given orders not to be disturbed by anyone."

"Well, isn't that just too bad." Manning pushed him roughly to one side, opened the door and went in.

Viner stood behind the bar pouring drinks into two glasses. The man who was sitting on one of the high stools was about six-feet tall and his fawn gaberdine jacket was stretched tightly across broad shoulders. He had a craggy, dangerous face with a scar under one eye and the blond hair was cropped.

Manning kicked the door shut behind him and there was a short, pregnant silence. "Why, Harry?" Viner said in a strained voice. "This *is* a surprise."

"I bet it is, you bastard," Manning said and moved forward.

An expression of real alarm appeared on Viner's face. "I don't know what you're talking about, but perhaps you'd better come back when you're reasonably sober."

Manning kicked a small coffee table to the other side of the room. "This is just the way I like it."

"Throw him out, Hans," Viner said.

"A pleasure, Herr Colonel," Hans replied and got to his feet.

Manning felt quite calm. It was as if he was somehow on the outside looking in on all this. He wondered about Hans. SS or Gestapo, one or the other, which led to interesting possibilities in Viner's past.

The German seemed very sure of himself. When he was about three feet away, he swung a tremendous punch that carried everything he had. To Manning, it was like a reed swaying in the wind. He moved in close, kicked him viciously on the shin and lifted his right knee into the unprotected face as Hans doubled over.

He lay on his back moaning, blood spurting from his smashed mouth and nose. "Get up, Hans! Get up!" Viner ordered.

"I don't think he's going to be quite that stupid." Manning took the Luger from inside his shirt, sat on one of the stools and reached across to tap Viner between the eyes with the hard, cold barrel. "It's no good getting on the radio to Rojas any more, Viner. I'm afraid I left him in a very sorry state."

"I don't know what you're talking about," Viner said, trying to speak calmly.

"You made sure they were waiting for me when I reached San Juan," Manning said. "You helped to murder Maria. I should put one in your belly right now, Viner."

"Please, Harry," Viner said desperately. "I'm only a tool. I have to do as I'm told. They have a hold on me, these people."

"What kind of a hold?"

"I was a colonel in the SS during the war. There is a warrant out for me from the War Crimes Tribunal at Ludwigsburg about a certain incident. Not a shred of truth in it of course, but you know what these witch-hunts are like."

Manning shook his head. "I'm tired of being pushed around, Viner. This is where it stops. Those bloody Cubans took me for everything I had in Havana. Well, upstairs in my room I've got someone they'd pay a lot more than my business was worth to get back. Am I right?"

Viner hesitated, obviously on the point of denying all knowledge of what Manning was talking about and then he cracked. "Yes, damn you."

"I thought you'd know all about it," Manning said. "Now this is what I'm going to do. Orlov isn't too happy about being here in case the authorities try to hold onto him, but I've promised to help. He trusts me."

"Ah, I see now," Viner said. "You'd be willing to make a deal?"

"With either you or the Russians. It's all one to me."

"How much?"

"One hundred thousand dollars American, and it's cheap at the price."

"It would take me some time to contact my principals."

Manning shook his head. "Nothing doing. Either I meet the boss man myself or the whole thing's off."

Viner shrugged. "Suit yourself, but we must go after dark."

"How far?"

"Two hours' run, no more."

"One of the cays off Exuma?"

Viner smiled. "My dear Harry, do you take me for a fool?"

"Not exactly."

"Very well. We'll go in your boat. I'll meet you at the jetty around eight oclock."

"Fair enough," Manning said, "but Orlov stays here with Seth. They're my insurance against you trying to pull something on me out there."

"What about a crew?" Viner said.

Hans was sitting up, holding his face and moaning slightly. Manning nudged him with his toe. "Laughing boy here should be fit enough by then."

As he reached the door, Viner said, "What about Morrison? He's still here?"

"I know," Manning said. "I've just seen him. I told him Garcia was dead. That I was lucky to be back here in one piece."

"You didn't mention me?"

"No, but I could do; remember that."

He closed the door, pushed his way through the crowd and went back upstairs. Orlov was sitting on the edge of the bed in a bathrobe and Morrison stood at the window.

They both turned expectantly and the Russian said, "Well, what happened?"

"Nothing much," Manning said. "I've agreed to sell you, that's all."

"You've agreed to what?" Morrison demanded.

"I'm going to do a deal with Viner's friends. I'm meeting him on the jetty at eight. We're going to their headquarters in my boat."

"Did he say where?"

Manning shook his head and pulled off his shirt. "Two hours' run. That would take us down to the cays north of Exuma or the other side of Cat Island. No way of knowing."

"How do you know they won't cut your throat as soon as they get their hands on you?"

"Orlov stays here, so does Seth. Viner provides me with a deck-hand. You've nothing to worry about. I put on a pretty convincing display. I asked for a hundred grand and he didn't even blink."

Morrison was already moving towards the door. "I've got things to do if we're going to get this set-up in time."

Manning paused in the doorway to the bathroom. "Get one thing straight, Morrison. This is going to work. If you try bringing in the Navy or extra police, they'll smell a rat and we'll lose out."

"I've still got to get things alerted in Nassau so we can move in on this place as soon as we know where it is."

"See that's all you do," Manning told him and he went into the bathroom and turned on the shower.

16

Greek Fire

It was the slight breeze lifting in from the sea that brought him awake so gradually that he lay there in the cane chair on the balcony, only half-conscious, not quite sure of where he was.

He was naked except for a towel about his waist and he shivered slightly and swung his legs to the floor. The heat of the day was over and the sun was dropping towards the horizon.

He paused just inside the french windows, listening to the Russian's steady breathing, and then walked silently across the carpeted floor to the wardrobe, took out fresh clothes and started to dress. As he fastened his belt, the phone buzzed sharply.

"Manning here," he said in a low voice.

"Reception, Mr. Manning. There's a young lady to see you. A Miss Melos."

"Tell her I'll be right down."

Orlov still slept steadily and Manning pulled on a linen jacket and left the room, closing the door quietly behind him.

Anna was sitting on a divan near the door, leafing through a magazine. She was wearing a sleeveless linen dress that fitted her perfectly and her long black hair hung in a pigtail over one shoulder.

"Hello, Anna," he said.

She stood up and smiled shyly, obviously at a loss for words. "Hello, Harry."

The band started to play in the dining room and he grinned. "Eaten yet?"

She shook her head. "I don't believe I have. I slept for a few hours. When I awoke, the only thing I was sure of was that I *had* to see you."

"The food here's marvellous. Anything you've got to say can wait till you've sampled it."

Although it was early, several couples were already dining and the head waiter moved across with a smile. "Booth or ringside, Mr. Manning?"

"We'll take a booth, I think," Manning said and they followed him between the tables.

When they were seated, he waved the menu away. "I don't need to see that. We'll have green turtle soup, salt pork with herbs, followed by baked bananas in brandy. Two iced vodkas to start with."

Anna smiled and shook her head. "You know what you want in everything, don't you?"

"Good Nassavian cooking, that's all. How's your father?"

"Much better. He wanted to come himself, but I wouldn't let him."

"If it's about the boat, you're wasting your time. I'll have the papers drawn up, first chance I get."

She shook her head. "We can't take her, Harry. In the first place, she's five times the boat the *Cretan Lover* ever was and I've been talking to Seth. He told me a lot of things. The *Grace Abounding* is all you've got left in the world."

"Which puts me in the same position as your father, except for one important different. He's an old man, I've still got a few years left."

She shook her head. "I know my father. He has pride. He won't take the boat. He likes you too much."

"You blasted Greeks are all the same," he said. "From Odysseus down. That boat's going to Harmon Springs whether he likes it or not. After tonight, it'll be his and that's an end to it."

"After tonight?" she said with a slight frown. "What do you mean?"

"I'm going on a little trip with Viner. Couple of hours there, couple of hours back. Nothing much."

She leaned across, her face quite pale. "You're running your head into a noose again."

He grinned wryly. "What have I got to lose?"

At that moment, the soup arrived and he deliberately altered the whole trend of the conversation. She had a healthy appetite and he found himself watching her covertly at every opportunity.

He ordered coffee, excused himself and went upstairs to Morrison's room. The door was locked. He knocked softly, but got no reply. When he went downstairs again, he paused beside the reception desk to light a cigarette, and glanced at the board. Morrison's key was on its hook and he returned to the dining room.

The band had started to play again and as he approached the table, he held out his hand and smiled. "How about it?"

She stood up and they moved on to the small dance floor. She slipped an arm around his neck and danced with her head on his shoulder, her firm young body so closely pressed against him that he could feel the line from breast to thigh.

When the music stopped, they stayed together for a brief moment and then she pulled gently away. "It's hot in here."

"Cooler outside," he said.

A path through the gardens at the rear took them out of town through casuarinas and a grove of palm trees planted by some early settler years before. They came out on the edge of a cliff that dropped to a white strip of beach.

The sea was black with depth, purple and gray near the shore and the sun was a ball of orange fire already drowning. The beauty of it was too much for a man and Manning felt sad and drained of all emotion. She turned and looked at him in a strange, remote way and he took one of her hands. They went down the broad path to the beach together.

Manning paused to light a cigarette. When he looked up, she turned slowly and stared at him never more lovely, the strange light playing across her face. She whispered his name once and stumbled towards him and they came together naturally and easily at the water's edge. Her hands pulled his head down as her mouth sought his and he lifted her in his arms and carried her up the beach. When he laid her down in the hollow between two rocks, her face was wet with tears.

As they went through the palm trees and down through the gardens into town, they walked hand-in-hand. Her dress was stained with salt water and badly crumpled. She paused to examine herself in the light from a window.

"I'll have to change as soon as we get back. I don't want to shock my father in his old age."

She smiled delightfully and Manning was filled with a sudden rush of tenderness. "Any regrets?"

She shook her head gravely. "What about you?"

He smiled and reached out to touch her face. "What do *you* think?"

They took a short cut through the gardens at the back of one of the hotels. He could hear the splash of water from a fountain hidden amongst the bushes and the air was heavy with the scent of night, filling him with an aching longing for something that was always out there beyond the darkness, never close enough to touch.

He paused to light a cigarette and she turned, her face revealed for a few seconds only as the match flared. She gazed at him steadily, her eyes reflecting the light so that

132

it was impossible to see beneath the surface. When he spoke, he realized that out of some strange instinct she had sensed his mood.

She placed a hand on his arm, holding him for a moment. "What happened back there—it didn't mean a thing. As far as I'm concerned, you're as free as you ever were."

"I know, Anna. I know."

He had the feeling she expected more, but there was nothing he could think of. At least nothing that would have reassured her. They continued their way in silence.

The Caravel was a blaze of lights, the sound of voices and carefree laughter echoing through the night, mingling with the gay, pulsating rhythm of the *goombay.*

They paused at the bottom of the steps leading up to the entrance. "I'll only be a couple of minutes," he said. "I want a word with Morrison."

In the strange distorted light thrown out by the Chinese lanterns that swung from the branches of the sea-almond rees, it was impossible to analyse her expression and yet he knew that, in some strange way, she had stepped firmly away from him.

"I'll go on ahead," she said. "We won't have much time to get ready."

He tried to think of something to say, but nothing would come to mind. What did she want with him, this dark, lovely girl? What had happened had been in another time, another place. Better to leave it like that.

"I'll see you down there then," he said and she turned and merged with the darkness.

He paused at the reception desk for some cigarettes and noticed that Morrison's key still hung on the board. He went upstairs, a slight frown on his face, wondering what the hell the American was playing at.

He was still frowning when he went into his room and turned on the light. There was no sign of Orlov. The coverlets on the bed had been pulled neatly into place and the French windows stood open to the night.

He went back downstairs and paused at the reception

desk again. "The gentleman who was sharing my room? Have you seen him this evening?"

"He went out about half-an-hour ago, sir."

Manning frowned, a tiny flicker of alarm moving inside him. "Was he on his own?"

The clerk shook his head. "Oh, no, sir. He was with Mr. Morrison, the American gentleman staying in 105."

Manning turned away, relief surging through him and went into the bar. He lit a cigarette and ordered a bar-cardi. As the barman brought it, Viner pushed through the crowd.

"On the house, George, and the same for me." He turned with a smile, supremely elegant in his white dinner jacket. "Ready to go, Harry?"

"Whenever you are."

"I've one or two things to settle up here. I'll see you on the jetty in about an hour as arranged." He raised his glass and a slight smile tugged at the corners of his mouth. "Let's hope you get what you're expecting at the other end."

"Don't worry about me," Manning said. "I'll make out."

He finished his drink, turned and pushed his way through the crowd. As he went down the steps into the cool night there was a slight frown on his face because for some obscure reason, Viner had appeared to be laughing at him and he couldn't think why.

There were lights in one or two boats, but the jetty was deserted. As he drew near to the *Grace Abounding* he could hear the radio. It was one of the many record shows that could be picked up from the States and of all things, they were playing *Valse Triste*.

He moved across the deck and paused in the shadows by the companionway, filled with that strange aching sadness again. As the record ended, he sighed and took a step forward. Someone planted a foot in his back that sent him stumbling down the steps. The door at the bottom swung open and he staggered into the cabin and fell on his knees.

He started to get up and a voice said, "Careful, Manning."

Hans stood behind the door, a sub-machine-gun in his hands. Anna, her father, and Seth sat on one side of the saloon, Orlov and Morrison on the other. A large, grim-faced Negro in red and white striped jersey lounged in the entrance to the galley. He was armed with a machine-pistol.

Manning stood up, arms raised and Hans ran an expert hand over him and found the Luger. He shoved it into his waistband, stepped back and Manning turned.

Kurt Viner was standing in the entrance to the companionway.

"And now perhaps we can get started?" he said.

17

The Green Light

As the *Grace Abounding* moved out of harbour and turned into the gulf, Manning glanced back over his shoulder and watched the lights of Spanish Cay fade into the darkness. For the moment, there was nothing to be done. The big Negro leaned in the corner of the wheelhouse, the barrel of his sub-machine-gun resting across his forearm and a third man squatted in the stern holding a rifle.

After a while, the door opened and Viner came in. "You can wait outside, Charlie. I don't think Mr. Manning will do anything foolish."

"I wouldn't be too sure about that," Manning said as the Negro moved out.

"Oh, but I am. Hans has orders to open fire at the first sign of trouble on deck. I'm sure you realize the damage even a single burst from his sub-machine-gun would inflict in the confined space of the cabin."

"So you win for the moment," Manning said. "Where do we go from here?"

Viner leaned over the chart table. "Jackson Cay, about ten miles off the southern tip of Cat Island. Do you know it?"

"I've been near it a time or two, that's all. I heard it was owned by some American millionaire."

"So it was a year or two back. Cigarette?"

There seemed no point in refusing and Manning leaned forward for the proffered light. The north-west trades blowing across the gulf carried some of the warmth of day through the open window. There was no moon and yet the sky seemed to be alive, aglow with the incandescence of millions of stars.

Viner breathed deeply, inhaling the freshness, and followed with his eyes a school of flying-fish as they curved out of the sea in a shower of phosphorescent water.

"You know, Harry, on a night like this it's good to be alive." He sounded as if he genuinely meant it.

Manning shook his head. "There are times when I'm almost convinced you're human."

"My dear fellow, there's nothing personal in any of this. I hope you realize that. You were foolish enough to get mixed-up in something that wasn't really any of your business and you've lost rather badly, that's all."

"Aren't you forgetting Maria and Jimmy Walker?"

Viner sighed and shrugged helplessly. "A regrettable necessity and certainly not of my choosing."

"I'll bet it wasn't. How did you get on to me so quickly?"

Viner's teeth gleamed in the darkness. "I've had Morrison's room wired for sound from the moment he arrived. I sat in my office and listened to every word you said to him. If you're hoping for help from Nassau you can forget it. I'm afraid he never even got out of the hotel after leaving you."

"And Orlov?"

"Quite simple. A phone call from the reception clerk

to say that you wanted him to meet you at the boat as soon as possible."

He was right. It had been simple. Too damned simple and Manning swallowed the black anger that erupted inside him and forced himself to consult the chart.

"You seem to have it all neatly worked out."

"I think so. Is there anything I've overlooked?"

"What happens at the other end?"

Viner smiled. "I'm afraid you'll have to wait for the answer to that one." He opened the door and said to Charlie, "Tell Paco I want him."

The Negro waved to the man in the stern who came forward at once. "What's the idea?" Manning said.

"It's a clear run to Jackson Cay now. Paco can take the wheel for a while. You can go back to your friends. I'll call you when I need you. Go with him, Charlie."

Manning walked along the deck and went below. Seth and Anna were making coffee and Hans sat against the wall beside the entrance to the gallery, his finger crooked in the trigger guard of his sub-machine-gun.

Manning ignored him and crouched beside Papa Melos. "How's it going, Papa?"

The old man looked better than he had done since San Juan. "I'll make out, boy. Don't worry about me."

Manning clapped Seth on the shoulder and moved across to Orlov and Morrison. "Anyone got a cigarette?"

Morrison produced a packet and held it out. "Rather battered, but still smokable."

He was very pale and Manning noticed a livid bruise on the side of his neck. "Looks like you got careless."

The American nodded. "For once."

Manning turned to Orlov. "What about you? Viner said anything?"

"The usual things. If I'm a good boy and do as I'm told, they'll make things easy for me."

"A fair offer under the circumstances."

"I know it is." Orlov sighed heavily. "The trouble is its always been a policy of mine never to go back to anything."

Seth brought the coffee in from the galley and Anna

followed with a plate of sandwiches. As she leaned across to put them in the centre of the table, Hans ran his hand up her leg. She turned and struck him blindly and he grabbed her wrist and twisted it, forcing her to one knee.

Before Manning could move, Orlov was on his feet. "Take your hands off her, you pig!"

He moved forward and Hans pushed the girl away and raised the sub-machine-gun. "Another step and I fill your belly."

"Go ahead!" Orlov laughed harshly and extended his arms. "Viner will like that. I'll be so useful when I'm dead."

The German's forehead was beaded with sweat and his tongue flickered over dry lips. "Sit down and shut up."

"Better do as he says, mister," Charlie called from the companionway. "I could always lay the barrel of this thing across the side of your head."

Orlov ignored him, extending his hand to Anna and sat her at the table. He smiled down. "No repetition, I promise you."

Manning was conscious of a sudden irrational jealousy as she smiled warmly at the Russian. And yet he had no right. No right at all. He went to the table for coffee and returned to his seat.

For a little while Orlov sat beside her and they talked in low voices and then he yawned, moved across to the other bench seat beside Seth and her father, and leaned back, eyes closed.

Manning folded his arms and let his head tilt forward. It was quiet in the cabin except for the rush of the water against the hull and he sat there feeling strangely fatalistic about everything. He was on a course already charted and there could be no going back. The ultimate end of things was something none of them could avoid.

Anna bowed her head on her arms. For quite some time he thought she was sleeping and then she turned her head sideways and opened her eyes. She stared at him unwinkingly, one arm still flat on the table shielding her from Hans. Very gently, she opened the map drawer with her free hand.

In that same moment Manning remembered the Smith & Wesson. He caught a brief glimpse of the revolver as she took it out and placed it on her lap. She unfastened the front of her dress, slipped the revolver inside and buttoned it again.

She stared at him steadily the whole time and fear moved inside him like a cold knife. He shook his head gently. For the time being, the gun was useless. If either Hans or Charlie had cause to open up with their sub-machine-guns, the cabin would be reduced to a bloody shambles within seconds.

A voice called down the companionway and Charlie got to his feet and nodded to Manning. "Mr. Viner wants you."

The deck was wet with spray and Viner stood at the rail looking across to the dim bulk of Cat Island. He turned as Manning approached.

"Not too long now, Harry. I'd like you to take over again. Paco has his limitations. I'll direct you when the time comes."

Manning went into the wheelhouse and the Cuban moved out. In spite of the fact that there was no moon, visibility was surprisingly good and he could clearly pick out each cay and island his finger moved to as he checked the chart.

They sailed between two small islands and beyond lay the larger bulk of Jackson Cay. Viner moved in from the deck. "You'll see an intermittent green light. Follow it in, but slowly. It's a narrow channel."

Manning reduced speed and coasted in towards the cay. There was a house high up on the clifftop and then he saw the green light winking through the darkness beneath it.

"We're getting pretty close to that cliff," he said.

"The channel runs into a large cave," Viner told him. "There's nothing to worry about. Just follow the light."

Rocks loomed high on either side, there was a sudden turbulence and then they passed in through a dark archway. The green light was fixed to the end of a stone jetty and was obviously operated by a timing device. There was only one other boat in sight, a forty-foot diesel launch painted cream with a red stripe running along the water-line. As Manning ran the *Grace Abounding* alongside, Paco jumped for the jetty with a line.

Manning cut the engines, moved out on deck and was immediately conscious of the terrible coldness of the damp air.

"After you?" Viner said and gestured over the rail.

As Manning stepped onto the jetty, the others came up from the cabin and joined him. A flight of stone steps lifted out of the gloom to a landing above their heads and he wearily mounted them at Viner's heels.

At the top, the German opened a door which led into a stone-flagged passage. He led the way to the far end, opened another door and climbed a short flight of steps which entered directly into a large hall.

It was tastefully furnished with carpets on the floor and dark oak-panelled walls. Viner opened another door and entered. There were two men in the room, both obviously Cuban. One sat at a short-wave transmitting set, earphones clamped to his head, the other was behind a desk writing. He got to his feet and smiled.

"So, you have managed to gather them all in?" he said in Spanish. "Any problems?"

Viner replied in the same language. "It was really quite simple, my dear Vargas. We got the American before he was able to communicate with British Intelligence in Nassau. Does the colonel wish to see them?"

Vargas shook his head. "Only Señor Manning. For the time being, the others can go below. See to it, will you?"

As Viner turned and gave Hans and Charlie the necessary orders, Vargas moved across the room and opened another door, went inside and closed it. A few moments later, he returned.

"This way, Señor Manning."

As Manning moved forward, Viner made to follow him and Vargas shook his head. "Not necessary, Viner. The colonel wishes to see Señor Manning alone."

Viner shrugged and turned away and Manning went inside. As the door closed behind him, he had a brief impression of a large, comfortable room, the walls lined with books and a fire that crackled cheerfully on a wide stone hearth.

In that same moment, the walls started to undulate and he breathed deeply, fighting the darkness that moved in on him, threatening to drive every last shred of sanity out of his mind. But when the mist cleared, he found that his eyes hadn't deceived him.

It was Maria Salas who sat behind the desk on the far side of the room.

18

The Purpose of Terrorism
Is to Terrorize

Behind her, the wall was of curved glass and he was aware of little things. The sound of the sea rushing in across the rocks, the scent of hibiscus from the garden.

"Better have a drink, Harry," she said. "You look as if you could do with it."

There were several bottles and glasses on a side table and he helped himself to a large rum. He emptied the glass in one quick swallow, filled it again and turned to look at her.

She wore a military style drill shirt open at the neck and narrow khaki pants. Her hair was tied back with a red ribbon, the one concession to femininity, and her face was smooth and untroubled as she returned his gaze gravely.

"I must say you're looking remarkably healthy," he said, dropping into the chair on the other side of the desk.

"More than I can say for you," she replied. "Hardly surprising under the circumstances. A lot seems to have happened since we were last together."

"In bed as I recall," Manning said dryly. "Viner kept referring to a colonel when we were outside. Would that be you?"

"I'm a lieutenant-colonel of the Military Intelligence Special Executive of the Cuban Army," she said calmly. "Group-leader for the Bahamas."

"Since the beginning?" he said. "Since the day I picked you up out in the gulf in that refugee boat?"

"That's right."

"And Viner?"

"It was easy enough to draw him into the net after I discovered his background."

"And what about me?" he said. "Where did I fit in?"

"You also had your uses, Harry."

He frowned for a moment and then realized what she had meant. "Of course, good old Sanchez and the letters I passed on to him for your mother."

"One can't say everything over the radio," she said. "Not even in code."

He moved back to the side-table and picked up the rum bottle. "Just for the record, what really *did* happen that night you left?"

She took a cigarette from a silver box on the table, lit it and leaned back in her chair. "A combination of things. The assassination of Miguel de Rodriguez had been planned for several days. I was to have no connection with it myself."

"Which was why you used Garcia?"

"He was expendable. A traitor to his country who thought he could buy his way back again."

"Why the pretence that you were on the plane?"

She shrugged. "Things seemed to be warming up. We knew that Morrison was a C.I.A. man. When he arrived on Spanish Cay, I couldn't be sure that he wasn't on my trail. To die seemed the surest way to put him off the scent if he was. In any case, it was time for me to move on."

144

And then Manning began to see things more clearly. "You persuaded Jimmy Walker to help you?"

She nodded. "I told him that you were getting too serious, that I wanted to break away. That if you thought I'd left for Miami, you'd follow me there."

"So you never even got on the plane?"

She shook her head. "Poor Jimmy. He thought I'd be waiting for him at his beach cottage. He was going to fly me to Vera Cruz next day."

For a moment, Manning saw again the pale face, the hair waving gently in the green water. A spasm of anger moved inside him. "He loved you, Maria. Didn't that count for anything?"

"Miguel de Rodriguez had to die. He was an enemy of the state. A threat to every free Cuban."

"There were three other people in the plane. Did they have to go too?"

"A regrettable necessity. We must show our enemies that we mean business."

"So you butcher the innocent."

"The purpose of terrorism is to terrorize. That's the only way in which a small country can hope to defeat an Empire. Lenin said that."

"The latest catch-phase goes one better," Manning told her. "We will bury you." He was suddenly filled with disgust. "My God, they must have done a good job on you."

"They didn't need to," she said, filled with that same unnatural calm. "I work for the destiny of a nation. To achieve our end, any sacrifice is worthwhile."

And then the combination of the rum and the closeness of the room was too much for Manning and everything seemed to move in, to lose definition, as if nothing were real. It was as if he were outside all this, looking in on a wild nightmare that had no sense to it, no beginning or end.

"My father was a good man," she said. "A lawyer. He helped the poor and defended political prisoners when no other defense counsel could be found. When I was thirteen years of age, Batista's secret police came for him

145

one night. He never even reached police headquarters. They said he was shot trying to escape."

"I'm not going to defend Batista's régime," Manning said. "No reasonable person would, from the President of the United States downwards."

"Later on the same night, they returned to the house to look for documents," she continued. "Six of them took my mother into the garden. The soldier who had been left to guard me, broke into the liquor cabinet. When he had reached a suitable state of drunkenness, he raped me."

Her voice moved on, but Manning didn't hear. He closed his eyes and fought against an agony that was almost physically, a hard ball that rose in his throat, threatening to choke him. He lurched across to the side-table, poured ice-water into a glass and swallowed it quickly.

When he turned, there was a look that might almost have been compassion on her face. "It's of no consequence, Harry. It happened a long time ago."

He shook his head. "It might be happening tonight. Do you think the D.I.E.R. act any differently from Batista's secret police? Castro's kept everything that was rotten in the old régime and added to it."

She jumped to her feet, her face flushed with anger. "You will not say things like that. I refuse to allow it. I was in the mountains with Fidel. He is a great man."

"The colonel refuses to allow it so that makes everything all right," he said softly.

She went out through the french windows and, after a moment, he followed her. She was standing by the rail and he moved beside her. The immediate sensation was that they were floating in space. The darkness was perfumed with the scent of flowers and the great bowl of night dipped to meet the sea, stars glittering into infinity.

"What happens now?" he said.

"You will be returned to San Juan, all of you."

"To stand our trial for crimes against the state?"

She shook her head. "That will not be possible."

"But of course," he said. "There's Orlov to consider. What a pity you can't have one of those really democratic

146

trials they like so much in Havana these days. Set the court up in the ball park, just to let everyone see that justice is being done."

"You will get your trial," she said. "There is justice for all in Cuba today."

The fanaticism, the sincerity in her voice was something he couldn't fight. He sighed and shook his head. "You win, Maria. When do we move?"

"Tomorrow evening. We will all be leaving together. Our task force will be done."

"Not before time. From what Morrison tells me, you've been pushing the action a little hard lately. From now on I think you'll find that things warm up considerably."

"By then it will be too late," she said. "Far too late."

In spite of her calmness, there was an edge to her words, a deeper meaning that he couldn't ignore.

"There's such a thing as taking the pitcher to the well too often."

"The tracker stations?" she shook her head. "This time we are after bigger game."

"And what might that be?"

She smiled for the first time since he had entered the room that night. "Dean Rusk and Lord Home."

The whole world seemed to stop breathing. He stared down into that calm, resolute face and in a movement that was purely instinctive, his hands reached for her throat.

She made no move to defend herself, but there was a sharp click as a gun was cocked and a tall, swarthy Cuban in a seaman's jersey stepped out of the shadows carrying a machine-pistol.

Manning dropped his hands and she shook her head. "Do you think me a fool, Harry?"

She turned without waiting for an answer and went back into the room. He stayed there for a moment and stared into the darkness, considering the enormity of the thing she contemplated. When he finally went in, she was sitting down again.

He moved around the desk and faced her. "You'll never get away with it, Maria. No one could get through the kind of security net those two will have around them."

"With careful planning, anything is possible." She opened a drawer, took out a chart and spread it on the desk. "Here is Nassau and fifteen miles away is Lyford Cay where Rusk and Home are to meet. At two o'clock tomorrow afternoon, they're going for a short cruise in a diesel yacht. At three, they anchor beside a red buoy specially positioned in the channel and watch an exhibition of water ski-ing. There is nothing we don't know about their movements."

"And you think they'll let you get close enough to try anything?" Manning said.

"We don't even need to be here," she replied patiently. "At dawn tomorrow, I'm going skin-diving off Lyford Cay."

"At dawn?" he said, frowning, "I don't understand."

"You will, Harry, I assure you. It'll be in all the papers." She pressed a buzzer on the desk and immediately, the door opened and Vargas entered. "I've finished with Señor Manning. You can put him with the others."

Manning took a step towards her. "Maria, for God's sake, listen to me."

But he was wasting his time. The man on the terrace moved in and Maria pulled a sheet of paper forward and picked up a pen. Manning turned abruptly, brushed past Vargas and went into the other room.

Viner was sitting on the edge of the desk smoking a cigarette. He smiled faintly. "Life's just full of surprises isn't it, Harry?"

Manning ignored him and helped himself to a cigarette from a packet on the desk. "She's crazy. You all are if you think you can get away with this."

Viner gave him a light. "I think you may be surprised, Harry. It's really a very good plan."

"It'll need to be."

The man with the machine-pistol poked him with the barrel and he moved out through the door, Viner at his shoulder. They crossed the hall and descended a flight of stairs at the back of the house.

There was a large, whitewashed wine cellar at the bottom, brightly lit by a naked electric bulb. Viner's two men, Paco and Charlie, squatted on the floor and played cards, their sub-machine-guns propped against the wall.

Paco jumped to his feet and took a bunch of keys from his pocket. "Where shall I put him?"

"With his friends, by all means." Viner said pleasantly. "You'll find them all there, Harry, except for your girl-friend. She's got a cellar all to herself. Maria is surprisingly puritanical about such things."

They moved past several doors, heavily barred with iron, a small grille set in each. Manning caught a brief glimpse of Anna's white face and then they paused at the next door. When it was opened, there was a confused impression of faces and then he was pushed inside and the door clanged shut.

He ignored the rush of questions and peered through the grille, watching Viner walk away. Suddenly, he laughed harshly and turned to face them.

"For God's sake, what is it, Harry?" Morrison demanded.

"One of life's little ironies," Manning said. "It's just occurred to me that two great men are going to die because a drunken peasant raped a little girl seventeen long years ago."

19

The Stern Sea Chase

It was bitterly cold and Manning sat against the wall and smoked one of Morrison's cigarettes. Seth and Papa Melos both appeared to be dozing and Orlov stood at the grille and peered outside. Morrison paced restlessly up and down.

After a while, he crouched beside Manning. "If I don't get out of here soon, I'll go crazy."

"That kind of talk won't get us anywhere. What time is it?"

Morrison peered at the luminous dial of his watch. "Two a.m."

"They'll be leaving soon," Manning said. "Have to if they want to be off Lyford Cay by dawn. It's a three-hour run."

"What are they going to do when they get there, that's what I want to know?"

"Perhaps they intend to plant a mine in the channel. That would fit in with her remarks about not being there when it actually happened."

"But plenty of craft use that channel," Morrison said. "I've never heard of a mine yet that could select its victims." He jumped to his feet. "God, it makes me go cold all over just to think about it. Don't these crazy fools realize what they're doing? Lighting the fuse to another war. No one's ever going to believe the Cubans pulled this one on their own."

"Perhaps that's exactly what they want. It would certainly force Russia's hand."

"And we're cooped up here," the American said. "What I wouldn't give for a gun right now."

"Anna's got one," Manning told him. "I saw her take my Smith and Wesson from the chart drawer when we were on the boat."

"Then why in hell hasn't she used it?"

"I'm glad she's had the good sense not to try. It wouldn't go very far against a sub-machine-gun, or would you like to try your luck?"

"Under the circumstances, I believe I would."

Manning turned to Orlov, who had been keeping the guards under constant observation. "What's happening out there?"

"Nothing much. They've got a bottle of whisky. Must have drunk half of it between them. The Negro can stand it better than Paco."

"Have they said anything interesting?"

Orlov shrugged. "The usual things. Their experiences with women and so on. Paco seems to have taken a fancy to Anna. The Negro's just been pointing out how unpleasant the consequences would be if the colonel ever found out he'd touched her."

"Thank God for that," Manning said and at that moment, a step sounded on the stairs.

As he went to the grille and peered out, Viner entered and spoke to Charlie, who hastily picked up his sub-machine-gun and went upstairs. The German walked across and stopped just outside the door.

"I thought I'd let you know that we're leaving now, Harry. No need to worry. We'll be back before noon."

"I wouldn't count on that," Manning said and the German chuckled and walked away.

A few minutes later, Manning heard the dull rumble of diesel engines breaking into life. When the muffled throbbing faded into the distance, a sudden unnatural quiet descended. Paco produced the whisky bottle which he had hurriedly hidden on Viner's entrance and held it to his lips.

Manning turned and sat down beside Morrison. "For God's sake give me a cigarette."

As they sat there in the darkness, he felt the strength drain out of his tired body. There was nothing they could do. Nothing at all—and then Paco started to sing.

He was very drunk. As they crowded the grille to watch him, he placed the neck of the bottle to his lips and laughed as whisky slopped over his face and shirt.

When the bottle was empty, he smashed it against the wall, staggered across the floor and stood swaying in front of Anna's cell.

"*Querida,* my little darling. Be nice to Paco. Come out."

Manning's hands gripped the bars tightly and he struggled to hold back his rage. Sweat mingled with the whisky, trickling over the fat, foolish face. Paco laughed suddenly, fumbled in his pocket and produced the bunch of keys.

"But of course. How foolish of me."

Anna hadn't uttered a sound and he lurched forward to unlock the door. It crashed back against the wall, the iron facings ringing against the stone and he moved inside.

Anna called out something unintelligible and he gave a cry of rage. A moment later, she stumbled out of the cell. Her dress was torn from the shoulder to the waist, but she held the Smith and Wesson in her right hand. As Paso came after her, she turned, flung up her arm and shot him through the head.

He must have died instantly and she stepped over his body without looking down and pulled the bunch of keys from the door. It took four attempts before she found the right one and her fingers trembled slightly. As the lock clicked, she glanced up. For one brief moment Manning looked through the grille into her eyes and then he was outside and running across the cellar.

He picked up the sub-machine-gun, cocked it and moved to the bottom of the stairs. The swarthy Cuban who had been on the terrace outside Maria's room was already halfway down, his machine-pistol ready. Manning jumped back, poked the barrel of the sub-machine-gun round the wall and fired. The Cuban screamed and pitched head-first down the stairs, somersaulting into the cellar.

Morrison picked up the machine-pistol. "Now what?"

"There's a radio transmitter in a room off the hall. Want to try for it?"

"Sounds like a good idea."

Manning went up the stairs on the run and peered cautiously round the corner. The hall was deserted and he waved on the others. As they joined him, he crossed quickly to the door of the room containing the transmitter. Morrison joined him, standing on the side. Manning turned the handle gently and flung the door open.

The man at the transmitter was alone. As he turned in alarm, Morrison moved inside. "Do as you're told and you won't get hurt."

The Cuban didn't hesitate. His hand grabbed for the automatic on the desk beside him, giving Morrison no choice. He loosed off a burst that spun the man round, smashing the set in a dozen places.

At the same moment, heavy firing broke out from the far end of the corridor. As Manning turned to reply, bullets peppered the wall. Papa Melos gave a cry of pain and clutched his arm.

"Get them out of here," Manning yelled to Orlov. "Try for the boat. We'll cover you."

He fired a long burst as a head peered round the wall at the end of the corridor. Behind him. Orlov and Seth dragged the old man away, Anna running ahead of them.

A few moments later, the Russian called from the open doorway. Manning and Morrison fired together, backing slowly, then turned and darted into safety.

The door bolted on the inside and they followed the others down through the cellars until they came out on the steps that gave access to the jetty. The green light still blinked monotonously and the *Grace Abounding* rocked slightly in the water as waves slapped in through the entrance to the cavern.

As they went down the steps, a heavy pounding sounded on the door behind them. Orlov and Seth lowered the old man gently to the deck and Manning tossed his sub-machine-gun to the Russian and ran into the wheelhouse.

As the engines rumbled into life, there was a sudden cry and several men appeared at the top of the steps. Manning took her away with a surge of power as they started to fire. A bullet shattered one of the glass panels in the wheelhouse, showering him with splinters, and Orlov and Morrison fired in reply. A moment later, they were moving out to sea.

There was a heavy swell running and spray surged in through the shattered window, soaking his head and shoulders. The coldness of it and the taste of the salt on his mouth filled him with new life and he gradually took the engines up to full power.

The door banged open and Seth entered. "I've given her a quick check, Harry. Can't see any damage to the hull. The wheelhouse seems to have caught it worst."

"How's the old man?"

"Could be worse. Bullet passed clean through his forearm. His daughter and Mr. Orlov, they're fixing him up fine."

"What about Morrison?"

"He's trying to raise Nassau on the radio. Last I saw, he wasn't having much success."

Manning flicked on the chart light and leaned over. Immediately, bright spots of blood splashed across the chart and Seth gave an exclamation of dismay.

Manning put a hand to his face and winced, suddenly aware of the pain. A splinter of flying glass had sliced across his cheek.

154

"I'll get you a plaster from the first-aid box," Seth told him and went out on deck.

Manning leaned over the chart again, fixed their position and plotted a course quickly. As he finished his calculations, Morrison came in.

"Any luck with the radio?"

The American shook his head. "I've just had a look inside. Couple of valves missing. Somebody was obviously playing it very safe. What happens now?"

"That's up to you. I've chartered a course for Lyford Cay which passes about fifteen miles east of Johnstown Harbour. If I altered course, you could always raise Nassau from there."

"And bring them out into the open?" Morrison shook his head. "I'm not too happy about that and I'm not keen on wasting time in altering course. I've got an uneasy feeling they might get up to something. I think we should keep after them."

"I agree," Manning said. "If the weather stays like this, we stand a fair chance of catching up before dawn. We should certainly get there before they've finished whatever it is they intend doing."

"Are you sure about that? They've got nearly an hour's start on us, remember."

Manning touched the side of the wheelhouse lightly with one hand. "I've been concerned with boats since I was a boy, Morrison. You name it, I've sailed on it. The *Grace Abounding* is the finest craft I've ever known. She'll get you there."

Seth came in at that moment and cut into the conversation. "Take the wheel for a moment, Mr. Morrison, while I fix him up."

Manning sat down and turned his face to the light. Seth swabbed it quickly with a piece of lint soaked in antiseptic and affixed a plaster along the deep cut.

"Good as new," he said.

Manning took over the wheel again and Morrison lit a cigarette. "What if they're already on the job when we get there? She told you she was going skin-diving, remember."

155

"We'll go down after them." Manning turned to Seth. "You can break out all the diving equipment and check it. How about aqualungs?"

"We got three, but I ain't sure about spare bottles and Mr. Morrison used one for an hour the other day."

"Better check and let me know how things stand."

Seth nodded and went out and Morrison leaned over the chart to trace their course with a nervous finger. He looked up, face strained and anxious. "If we do have to go down after them, things could get nasty."

Manning shrugged. "Can you think of a better way of handling it? Out in the open and official, it would be the biggest international stink since the Cuban crisis."

Morrison nodded. "You're right, this is the only way."

"Of course I'm right." Manning grinned. "Go and give Seth a hand with the equipment and stop worrying."

The wind kicked spray against the window and he rubbed the weariness from his eyes and sat down, the wheel gripped tightly in his hands. There was no moon, but visibility was excellent and he strained his eyes into the distance. The door opened and Orlov entered.

"How's Papa Melos?" Manning said.

"Indestructible. He's having a sleep."

"Thank God for that. He's been hurt enough by this business."

"So, the stern sea chase begins?"

Manning glanced at him quickly. "You've been talking to Morrison?"

The Russian nodded. "I'd like to make up the party if you have to go down. I'm a useful man with an aqualung."

"How useful?"

Orlov shrugged. "The study of marine life is a sideline of mine. I've been at it for five years or so now. Mostly in the Black Sea, but I've put in a lot of time underwater since my posting to Cuba."

Manning grinned. "Looks like you're elected."

Orlov smiled charmingly. "I'm so glad you agree. I'd have insisted on going anyway. I'll take over for an hour if you like. Anna's got the coffee going below."

Manning didn't even try to refuse. His eyes were sore

and the nagging pain in his face seemed to drag him down. He went along the deck and paused at the rail for a moment before going below.

Seth and Morrison had the diving gear spread out on the floor and table of the saloon. There were a couple of brand new spear guns and Manning picked one up and frowned.

"Where did these come from?"

"Mr. Morrison bought them while you were away."

"What about spare bottles?"

Seth shook his head. "Not too good. About forty minutes for one of the aqualungs, that's all."

"Should be ample." Manning turned to Morrison. "By the way, Orlov's coming with us if we have to go down. Apparently he's something of an expert."

"So he informed me," Morrison said. "He's quite a guy, that Russian."

"An understatement," Manning said.

He moved into the galley as Anna came out of the forward cabin. Her face was white and strained and there were dark circles under her eyes.

"You look terrible," he told her. "You ought to get some sleep."

She poured coffee into a cup for him. "I heard Morrison and Sergei talking. I know what you're going to do. You mustn't."

He frowned. "I don't understand."

"Can't you see?" she said desperately. "You're making a personal issue out of this. She fooled you, that woman, and now you're going to risk your life again because your stupid vanity's been hurt."

She was close to tears and he shook his head slowly. "She doesn't mean a thing to me, not any more. As far as I'm concerned, Maria Salas was drowned off the Blackstone Reef five days ago."

She turned abruptly and fled into the cabin, shutting the door after her. Manning finished his coffee, went back into the saloon and stretched out on one of the bench seats.

Five days ago. Was that all? What was time, but events

turning endlessly in a circle that brought one to an ending that was ordained from the beginning of time. He closed his eyes and plunged into the dark waters of sleep.

20

Into an Indigo Dusk

The dawn came grey and cold with mist rolling in heavy patches across the water and the sea heaved in an oily swell. Seth was at the wheel and Manning stood beside him drinking hot coffee.

Under his denim pants and heavy sweater, he was dressed for diving, a heavy cork-handled knife at his belt, pressure-gauge and compass strapped to his wrists. He put down his cup, picked up a pair of binoculars and looked ahead.

"Not a damned thing. This would have to happen."

Morrison came along the deck wearing an old duffle coat, his face grey. "I thought they were supposed to be the sunny Bahamas?"

"So they are at the right time. Whoever saw a tourist up this early in the morning?"

The American glanced at his watch. "Five a.m. I'd forgotten there was such a time." He peered out anxiously into the grey mist. "Ten hours to zero."

Manning turned to the chart, worked out their dead reckoning based on miles logged and course sailed, and threw down the pencil.

"I'd say we're no more than a couple of miles south-south-west of Lyford Cay. Cut the engines, Seth."

He went out on deck as Anna and Orlov came up from the saloon. She was wearing one of his heavy sweaters, the sleeves rolled back. The Russian wore swimming shorts and a windcheater.

"Why have we stopped?" Anna said. "Are we there?"

Manning nodded. "Everybody quiet. Let's see if we can hear anything."

The boat lifted on the swell and then subsided and he stood at the rail listening intently. A seagull flew low over the deck and skimmed the water with a shrill cry and somewhere in the distance there was a rumble like thunder.

"What's that noise?" Orlov asked.

"Sea breaking over the reef closer to the cay," Manning told him.

Morrison was standing a few feet away, the binoculars to his eyes. He gave a startled exclamation and pointed ahead excitedly.

"I think I saw something. The mist seems to clear for a moment. About half-a-mile ahead."

Manning took the glasses and climbed on top of the wheelhouse. The wind was beginning to freshen, thinning the mist considerably in places. It would probably clear completely within an hour.

On the crest of a wave, he thought he saw a spar. The *Grace Abounding* dipped into a great hollow and then lifted high on the swell. As he focused the binoculars, the boat jumped at him through the ragged hole in the mist, the red band above the waterline contrasting vividly with the cream-painted hull. He took a rough fix with his wrist compass and jumped to the deck.

"She's there all right." He looked into the wheelhouse and gave Seth the new course. "Half-speed till I give you

160

the word. When we get close, let her have everything she's got and kill the engines as we drop across their stern." He turned to Morrison and Orlov. "We'd better get ready."

They went down into the saloon. Papa Melos was sitting at the table drinking coffee, his right arm in a sling. Manning opened the chart drawer, took out a box of .38 cartridges and and tossed it across to Morrison.

"You take the Smith and Wesson and stay in the wheelhouse with Seth in case things turn sour." He glanced at Orlov. "What about the other guns?"

"A couple of good bursts left in each, that's all."

"Then we'll have to make sure they count. When we hit, you go over for'ard. I'll jump from the stern."

He picked up his sub-machine-gun. As he turned, Anna laid a hand on his arm. "What about Papa and me?"

"You stay down here," he said. "And I mean that. We've enough to worry about up top."

She waited for a word, some sign, but he gave her none. The fingers that gripped his arm so tightly relaxed and she turned away.

"Don't worry about us, son," Papa Melos said. "We'll be fine."

Manning went up the companionway quickly and passed along the deck to the wheelhouse. The sound of the engines was only a muffled gentle throbbing as they moved steadily forward.

He altered course a half-point and stood at Seth's shoulder, his eyes straining into the opaque mist. He was aware of a sudden gust of wind through the shattered window, the boat heeled a little and the grey curtain was snatched away.

The Cuban boat was a couple of hundred yards to starboard, her colours standing out vividly against the grey morning. Behind her, the sea heaved over the reef, breakers and white water stretching into the mist. Manning slapped Seth on the shoulder.

The whole boat shuddered and lifted suddenly as the Negro took her forward at full power. The noise of the engines deepened into a steady roar and Manning ran along the deck to the stern, his sub-machine-gun ready.

A sailor in a black jersey stood in the waist of the Cuban ship, coiling a rope. As they emerged from the mist, he glanced over his shoulder and cried out in alarm. He ran along the deck and started to climb the short ladder to the wheelhouse.

Manning was aware of Orlov crouching at the rail, his machine-pistol ready, and then the gap seemed to shorten rapidly. Seth cut the engines and the *Grace Abounding* veered sharply to starboard as he swung the wheel, grazing the stern of the other vessel.

Manning went over the rail, slipped on the wet deck and stumbled to one knee. At the same moment, Charlie emerged from the companionway firing a machine-pistol from the hip. Manning caught him with a full burst that drove the Negro backwards into the cabin.

The engines coughed once as the man in the wheelhouse desperately tried to start them. Orlov ran along the windows with two short bursts. There was a terrible cry and the man collapsed in the doorway, one arm dangling down to the deck.

Manning approached the head of the companionway and called in Spanish, "Better come out."

Orlov joined him and stood on the other side of the door. "Last warning," Manning called.

A stream of bullets splintered the edges of the doorway and he jumped back out of harm's way. Orlov turned and vaulted over the rail onto the deck of the *Grace Abounding*. He dropped to his stomach, waited till the two vessels bounced a few feet apart in the heavy swell and emptied his machine-pistol through one of the saloon portholes. There was a sharp cry and the firing stopped abruptly.

He jumped for the deck of the Cuban ship and rejoined Manning. "Somehow I get the impression that's it."

"Which means we're too late," Manning said. "They're already on their way." He handed the sub-machine-gun to the Russian. "Cover me. I'm going down."

Charlie sprawled across the last half-dozen steps, his fingers hooked into talons. There was blood everywhere and Manning stepped across him into the saloon.

Viner lay on his face, his jacket charred and still smouldering, blood soaking steadily through. He had obviously received Orlov's final burst full in the back.

When Manning turned him over, the eyes were wide open and staring as if the German found difficulty in focusing properly. He moistened his lips and said faintly. "I told her she should have killed you before we left." He shook his head, an expression of wonderment on his face. "I can't believe it. Survival's become something of a habit with me since the war."

"Until Maria took a hand in the game," Manning said deliberately.

"The point hasn't escaped me." The German closed his eyes in pain for a moment and then opened them again. "She's gone under the reef with Hans and three Cubans. There's a red buoy fixed in the channel on the other side where the yacht will anchor this afternoon. They're going to fix a charge to it."

"To the buoy? But how will they detonate it? She said they wouldn't even be here when it happened."

"Radio beam from the boat's transmitter. Detonate it electronically from fifty or sixty miles away." Viner shook his head, an expression of puzzlement on his face. "What a way to go after all these years. Is there an answer, Harry?"

"Have a cigarette," Manning said. He lit one quickly, but as he took it from his mouth, the German's eyes closed and all that was left of life escaped from his body in a gentle sigh.

When Manning turned, Orlov and Morrison were standing in the entrance. "Did you get all that?"

Morrison nodded. "One thing puzzles me. He said they'd gone under the reef. What did he mean?"

They turned and went up on deck. "I know this place well," Manning said. "They call the reef 'The Cathedral'. It stretches for several miles to the south. A great passage cuts through for about three hundred yards, arched like a nave. On the other side in the channel, the reef slopes for a while and then goes down deeper than I've ever been."

They jumped for the deck of the *Grace Abounding* and started to strip.

"How long do you figure it'll take us to get round to the other side in the boat?" Morrison demanded.

"At least half-an-hour, it's tricky navigating," Manning said. "We'll be quicker if we go after them through the reef. Seth can take the boat round the long way and pick us up at the buoy."

Seth brought the aqualungs up on deck quickly and they struggled into them. One of Manning's straps twisted at the back. He tried to reach it and failed and Anna came across.

As he tightened his chest strap, she did the same for him at the sides. She picked up his diving mask and handed it to him. Her face was quite calm, the eyes steady. For a moment only, her fingers touched his and stayed there, and then she turned and joined her father who had come up on deck and now stood beside the wheelhouse with Seth.

Manning and Morrison had a spear gun each and Orlov had lashed one of the spare harpoons to the end of a six-foot boat hook, making it into a crude spear.

When they were ready, Manning nodded to Seth. "Allowing for the mist, you should reach the buoy in about half-an-hour. We'll see you there."

There was somehow a comfort in making such a definite statement and he went over the rail quickly and sank down into the cold waters.

In the dawn light, the sea was a place for grey-green shadows and he waited for the others and then swam forward into a milky phosphorescent mist. The current sucked them in towards the reef and he dived with a quick flick of his fins, sliding smoothly down towards the great arched opening they called The Nave.

It stretched into infinity, light slanting through the coral, shading already into different colours, adding to the illusion that they were swimming through some great submerged cathedral.

There was as yet no sign of their quarry, but already

the water was beginning to change colour and a few minutes later, he was aware of the turbulence of conflicting currents and they passed out into the channel.

When he surfaced, he saw the buoy at once, a red blob in the sea some three hundred yards away. He took a quick fix with his compass and submerged again. Morrison and the Russian were waiting for him and he waved them on and took the lead.

The sea change was startling. Already, the greyness was fading and the range of visibility through the clear green water was excellent. The reef slanted away beeneath them to the left and he moved on through that strange, silent world, fish scattering to avoid him.

He saw them as if through the wrong end of a telescope, and yet quite clearly. The chain of the buoy dropping down to the sloping surface of the reef, the five figures grouped around it just below the surface.

He moved on at the same steady pace, his spear gun ready. Orlov and Morrison on either side. A moment later, they were seen. Immediately, three of the figures detached themselves from the group and swam towards them.

Manning had eyes only for the one in the middle. He resisted the temptation to fire too early and waited for him. The man paused, treading water, perhaps unnerved by the relentless approach. He discharged his spear gun in a cloud of silver bubbles and Manning jack-knifed to avoid it and fired his own as he passed underneath.

The harpoon penetrated the man's belly and his body bucked in an agony so violent, the gun was pulled from Manning's grasp. He was aware of Morrison struggling hand-to-hand with the man on his left, of Orlov thrusting at his adversary with his crude spear. He hesitated and then drove on towards the buoy.

Maria and Hans were clamping a bulky package into place. Her long hair floated around her in a dark cloud and undulated like a living thing when she glanced over her shoulder and saw him coming.

Hans drew a knife from the sheath at his belt and came driving on. Manning had his ready in his left hand. For a moment, it seemed they must collide and then he turned to one side, narrowly avoiding the clumsy thrust the German made at him.

He broke through to the surface and jack-knifed immediately. The German floated six feet below him, his head turning frantically from side-to-side. Manning came down on top of him. His right arm encircled the neck and he pushed the knife in under the ribs, penetrating the heart immediately.

The German bucked, his arms thrashing the water, giving the whole terrible scene an air of nightmarish horror. When Manning released him, the body dipped down towards the reef, twisting over onto its back.

He started to turn, was aware of a sudden vibration in the water and was spun round by a blow in his right shoulder. As his right hand reached for the harpoon, pulling it out, the pain surged through him and he caught his breath sharply, swallowing the agony.

Maria poised a few feet away, the gun in one hand, the harpoon dangling on its line. He knew then that she had recognized him and kicked sharply with his flippers and moved towards her.

She released the gun, turned and swam rapidly away from him. It was then he realized that he still gripped his knife firmly in his left hand. He dropped it and went after her.

Time, the world, everything that had happened had ceased to exist for him. He was hardly even aware of the pain that blossomed in his body or of the blood that drifted around him in a brown cloud.

She was twenty or thirty yards ahead when she went over the edge of the reef. He followed her without hesitation, descending vertically down the face of the great cliff, his eyes never leaving the slim figure in the white suit with the long black hair floating behind.

Once, he glanced at his pressure gauge and saw they were already one hundred and fifty feet deep. It was at this point that the delirium took possession of him, aggravated by his weakened state and the tremendous physical punishment his body had taken during the past few days.

All colours had faded as they descended into a great blue vault. He was too deep, he knew that and yet some terrible compulsion drew him on. It was as if she were determined to take him with her and he was powerless to resist.

He checked his pressure gauge again at two hundred feet and stretched out a hand as if to call to her, but he was wasting his time. The darkness moved in on him as the slim white figure disappeared down into the indigo dusk.

21

All Passion Spent

It was quiet when he awoke and he found himself in unfamiliar surroundings. He was lying in a narrow hospital bed and the walls of the small room and its furniture were painted white.

He tried to sit up and was immediately conscious of the dull ache in his left shoulder. The walls seemed to undulate and something whispered through the silence of eternity. He took a deep breath and tried to push himself up even further. The door opened and a nurse entered.

She was a stout motherly person with a pleasant face and large capable hands. She moved forward quickly and eased him back on the pillow.

"You mustn't do that. You mustn't even move."

A stranger answered her, someone who had no connection with himself at all. "Where am I?"

"You're in hospital in Nassau. You've been here for

three days. Just rest quietly. I'll get the doctor."

She went out of the room and he lay there trying to put the pieces together in the right order, but it was impossible. His whole body ached and there was a strange persistent buzzing in his ears that refused to go away.

A few minutes later, the door opened again and someone approached the bed. He opened his eyes and saw a brown, kindly face topped by iron-grey hair.

"My name's Flynn. I've been looking after you. How do you feel?"

"Bloody awful."

He produced an ophthalmoscope and examined Manning's eyes carefully. After a while he grunted and put it back in his pocket. "I don't think there's likely to be any permanent damage."

"What's been the trouble?"

"Nitrogen poisoning. The bends. When they brought you in here three days ago I wouldn't have given much for your chances. You'd lost a hell of a lot of blood. On top of that, you'd gone down too deep."

And then things clicked into place and for a moment, Manning was back there reaching out vainly towards the slim figure as it moved deeper into the dusky water.

"Can't you remember?"

"Only vaguely. At the time, it seemed to be happening to someone else."

Flynn nodded. "Nitrogen narcosis, the so-called drunkenness of the deep. The effect varies with the individual. In your weakened state, you didn't stand much chance of fighting it off. Good thing you had your friend Smith along."

"Smith?" Manning said blankly.

"The man who brought you up. We had to put him in the pressure tank as well when they got you here, but not for as long. It took ten hours' hard work to clear your system."

Orlov. It was the only possible explanation. Probably Morrison had decided it would be politic for the Russian to keep quiet about his real identity for the time being.

"When do I get out of here?"

169

"Good heavens man, not for a fortnight at the very least." Flynn chuckled. "Don't look so put out. I'll give your friend Morrison a ring as soon as I've finished my rounds. He's been haunting the place for the past few days."

After he'd gone, Manning lay staring up at the ceiling thinking about Maria Salas. She had chosen the manner of her going, turning from life quite deliberately because her own dark purpose had failed. In the quiet, he seemed to hear her voice, high-pitched and full of bravura, echoing a final *flamenco* as she vanished into the mist. But for the moment, he was conscious of nothing. Only of an emptiness, a coldness that moved inside him and couldn't be explained.

The door opened and Papa Melos came in. He was wearing pyjamas and a blue dressing gown and his right arm was in a sling. He sat on the edge of the bed and grinned with pleasure.

"I couldn't wait, boy. When the doctor told me you'd finally come round, I waited my chance and skipped out when the nurse wasn't looking. Anna said she'd let Seth know when she gets back to the boat. He'll probably be up later."

"Anna?" Manning said. "She's been here this morning?"

The old man looked immediately uncomfortable. "She's been here every day, Harry. She was visiting me when the doctor came in and told us you'd come round." He seemed to search for the right words. "Look, it ain't none of my business, but maybe you two had a row or something. Anna's got a lot of pride. She wouldn't go where she thought she wasn't wanted."

There was a short, awkward silence and Manning deliberately changed the subject. "How's your arm?"

"Fine, Harry, just fine." The old man grinned. "In fact everything is. They're going to give me a new boat. The best money can buy. Mr. Morrison said the Secretary of State insisted."

Manning reached out and clasped his hand. "I'm glad about that, Papa. Truly glad."

The door swung open and the large, middle-aged nurse

swept in. Papa Melos gave her one guilty look and got to his feet.

"I should think so," she said.

He grinned at Manning. "Reminds me of my mother. If she'd lived, God rest her, they'd have been around the same age."

He ducked under her arm into the corridor and she followed him, closing the door behind her.

She came back later and brought Manning something to eat. As she arranged the tray across his knees, he noticed some flowers in a vase at the window and asked who had brought them.

She smiled. "They were left by Miss Melos. She's brought fresh ones each day."

After she'd taken the tray away, he lay staring out at the morning sunshine, thinking about Anna. His senses seemed sharper, more acute than he had ever known them. He could smell the perfume of the flowers and was filled with an aching longing for her.

The door clicked quietly open and he turned eagerly. Sergei Orlov was standing there. He wore a well-cut, dark-brown suit in tropical worsted, and sunglasses.

"Mr. Smith I presume?" Manning said.

The Russian grinned, took off his glasses and sat on the edge of the bed. "Morrison will be up in a few minutes. He's talking to the doctor. How do you feel?"

"As if I shouldn't be here," Manning said. "They tell me you went down after me. Just for the record, what happened?"

"I finished off my man and followed you. I didn't like the way you were bleeding."

"All the way down?"

The Russian nodded. "I've been that deep before and it hasn't affected me particularly. In this case, we had to come up too quickly. That's what caused the trouble."

"And Maria?"

"She took her own way out. She was still going down when I reached you."

Manning pushed the thought away from him and asked

171

for a cigarette. The Russian gave him one and they sat there smoking in silence.

"What happens now?" Manning said after a while.

"To me?" Orlov smiled. "A most interesting situation. Officially, I'm quite dead. This opens up a fascinating range of possibilities."

"Such as staying on this side of the fence?"

The Russian grinned. "Why beat about the bush? To tell you the truth, I'm flying to Washington with Morrison in the morning. We've really only been hanging on to see if you'd pull through. He seems to think they might find something for me to do."

"I'm sure they will," Manning said dryly.

The door opened and Morrison entered. He sat on the other side of the bed and smiled. "What in hell were you trying to do? Frighten us?"

They shook hands and Manning said, "Papa Melos was here a little while ago. He told me about the boat. I'd like to thank you."

"He deserved it."

"I hear you're having company on the trip back."

"You mean Smith here?" Morrison grinned. "He finally came to his senses." He hesitated for a moment and carried on, "In a way, I'm here in sort of official capacity to thank you."

"No need," Manning said. "I went into this thing in the first place for personal reasons. You know that."

"Naturally, the whole business stays a secret. I must say the authorities here have handled things superbly in that way. Under the circumstances, my government expresses a very real regret that you can't be thanked publicly for what you've done. However, there *are* other ways. I've been asked to tell you that we intend to compensate you fully for the loss of your salvage business in Havana."

Manning could think of nothing to say and Morrison nodded to Orlov and stood up. "You look pretty tired, Harry. Try to get some more sleep. We'll see you again before we leave."

After they had gone, he lay staring out of the window.

So now he could start afresh. Now he would have not only the boat, but enough money to go into the salvage business again. The thought cheered him immensely and he threw back the bedclothes and swung his feet to the floor. When he walked across to the wardrobe, he felt as if he were floating.

His best tan gaberdine suit was on a hanger and there was clean linen and a pair of shoes, obviously brought in by Anna or Seth against the day he would be leaving.

The pyjama jacket he was wearing was light blue and he left it on in place of a shirt. It took him quite some time to get into the suit because of his injured shoulder and he simply buttoned the jacket in the middle, allowing the empty sleeve to dangle freely.

The corridor was deserted and he went down the stairs at the far end. On the ground floor, there seemed to be a great many people moving about, some in uniform, but many of them patients. He moved into a pleasant tiled foyer. Facing him was a wide glass door.

A uniformed porter was standing in the porch and he looked at Manning curiously. "Can I get you a cab, sir?"

Manning was about to say yes when he remembered that he had no money. He shook his head. "First day up. I could do with the exercise."

He realized he had made a bad mistake before he had gone fifty yards, but he kept on moving through the side streets towards the harbour, staying in the shade as much as possible.

Sweat ran down his face in rivulets, soaking through the pyjama jacket and his shoulder was beginning to hurt when he finally turned a corner onto the waterfront.

It was packed with jostling humanity and he moved into the crowd, trying to protect his injured shoulder as much as possible. Someone swung a basket against it and he stifled a cry and forced his way through to the stone wall at the edge of the wharf.

He could see the *Grace Abounding* about a hundred yards away round the curve of the harbour. Anna was standing in the stern dangling a bucket on a line into the waer. As he watched, she started to swab the deck.

A hand tugged at his sleeve and he looked down into the face of Twenty-two, the little Negro boy in the American football jersey who'd shown them where Garcia lived an eternity ago.

"Heh, mister, remember me?"

"I'm never likely to forget you." Manning pointed across to the *Grace Abounding*. "Go and tell the lady who's swabbing the deck of that boat that I'm sorry. This is as far as I could get under my own steam."

The boy looked completely mystified. "Is that all, mister?"

"Tell you what I'll do," Manning said. "After you've told her, wait for me on the boat. I'll bet you ten shillings it'll be worth it."

The boy darted into the crowd and was immediately lost to view and Manning sat on the wall. The heat was tremendous and he closed his eyes, fighting against the darkness that tried to move in on him. When he opened them again, Anna was standing a few feet away.

Her expression was a strange mixture of incredulity, dismay and anger. She rushed forward, took his handkerchief from his breast pocket and mopped the sweat from his face.

"You fool!" she stormed. "You stupid damned fool! What do you want to do? Kill yourself?"

He shook his head. "I'm trying to convince a stubborn Greek that I love her, that's all."

She sagged against him for a moment, holding onto his jacket, and he gently stroked her hair with his free hand.

"Is there a chance for us, Anna? Do you honestly think there's a chance?"

She looked up at him, her face vibrant and alive. "I know one thing, Harry Manning. If we don't try, we'll regret it for the rest of our lives."

She slipped an arm about his waist and together, they moved through the crowd towards the *Grace Abounding*.